G R JORDAN

Dagon's Revenge

An Austerley & Kirkgordon Adventure #3

First published by Carpetless Publishing in 2018

First edition

ISBN: 978-1-912153-22-0

Editing by Caroline Orr
Cover art by J Caleb Clarke

This book was professionally typeset on Reedsy.
Find out more at reedsy.com

To Janet,
For finding me space when I need it and continuing to sail this
river after all these years.

Contents

Acknowledgement

As always, to my Janet for pushing me ever forward in this writing journey. To my wonderful children for letting their Dad have space to write. That kid's novel is coming!

To Caroline for the edit and Jake for the magnificent covers.

To my writing friends, for all the encouragement, ideas and advice. Keep writing and producing!

To the fantastic American gentleman who misheard my friend's name and then sent a package to a certain Mr Austerley. Your error was a gaff of genius.

To my team at the station for keeping the day job such fun! And for the support on the days it wasn't.

To God who gave me this creative talent, may He watch over me like He watches over Kirkgordon.

The Homing Foot

There was a soft crunch underfoot and Kirkgordon looked down to see charcoal soil beneath. Amongst the occasional rocks, long sprouts of wild grass were growing, or rather, existing, for the grass didn't protrude like massed ranks of spearmen but instead had a lazy limpness to it. There were no trees, just miles of undulating small hills like those he had seen around Belfast. Drumlins, the good folk there called them, but their scenery was green and lush from the abundant rainfall. Here was just bleak.

Calandra's black leather jacket and dark jeans made her almost fade into the scenery. He watched her survey the land, the ponytail of her long black hair waving from side to side. Her beauty was out of place here but he was glad to have her along for the ride. It wasn't just her fighting skills, which were a match for anyone he knew, but also the comfort of a woman whom he fought hard to see as a close sister and not a potential lover. No matter the place, she always looked good.

"Does Mr Austerley know where we are?" asked Havers, letting Kirkgordon know that his whole party had crossed through the portal from the Russian countryside to... to... well, to here, wherever *here* was.

"Give me a minute," grunted Austerley. "Only just bloody arrived."

"Nefol, Cally – do a little scout and come back in five minutes. See if there's anything around here," ordered Kirkgordon.

"Or any*one*," said Havers.

Nefol, though only a slip of a girl at twelve years of age, nodded with a grimness that a child of her age should not possess. Although she was "functioning well" in Calandra's words, it was evident that her father's death was taking its toll. Kirkgordon had watched Father Jonah be burnt to ashes by Farthington's breath, and he still struggled to shake the image. But she didn't seem to have vengeance on her mind. Unlike Havers.

"Mr Kirkgordon, how do you intend to find our target if we don't know where we are?"

Havers hadn't been impressed when Ma'am gave me control of this mission, thought Kirkgordon. And he's going to snipe whenever he can. "Since when is Farthington our target, Mr Havers?" Kirkgordon sniggered to himself. Major Havers hated to be called a Mister. "This is a rescue mission for Alana. The moment we get her, we leave. It's my call all the way, Mr Havers. Remember that."

"And *you* remember what that bastard dragon did to the priest." Havers stepped away, pretending to survey the local area. Austerley tapped Kirkgordon on the shoulder.

"Getting out of here soon-as is a good idea, Churchy. I think I know where we are but I'm not one hundred percent certain. Look how wasted everything is. This place has seen the Elders at some point. This decay isn't natural."

"Indy, I just walked through a portal from Russia to here. I kinda left natural behind. Anyway, maybe when daytime comes it'll be easier."

"Churchy, this *is* daytime!"

"What?" Kirkgordon looked around. "But it's so dark."

"Can you feel the thickness in the air? Even that is decayed, full of pollution. I think nightfall is going to bring a proper darkness."

"How's the foot?" asked Kirkgordon, looking at the booted appendage.

"Sore. And too small. But there's something else."

Hell, thought Kirkgordon, this won't be good. First he loses his foot, blaming me for pinning it with an arrow before Farthington ripped it off his leg. Then he somehow magics a foot off a witch but it's too small and has gone ebony black as it's full of evil. Now what?

"The foot has been tingling," said Austerley, "ever since we arrived. Just tingling."

"Which means?"

"How should I know, Churchy? It's my first evil foot, dammit."

"So, where are we?" asked Kirkgordon, trying to give Austerley a chance to talk about something he did know.

"Well, it's hard to say in English, there's no translation. Closest is probably the Nether Lands."

"Holland? How is this Holland?"

"Hardly. In the scrolls buried deep in the vaults of the St Basil church of the Nazarene, deep set into the Andes, the name given is—"

Kirkgordon heard the noises but they were not like any language he knew. Deciding not to ask for a linguistics lesson from Austerley, Kirkgordon changed tactics.

"So you know about this place. Good, Indy, we're going to need it. What can you tell me about it?"

"Not much," said Austerley, and Kirkgordon's face fell. "But

I wouldn't holiday here."

But Austerley would go anywhere to look at this occult stuff, thought Kirkgordon. We must be in trouble.

Calandra emerged from behind a small hillock and raced up to Kirkgordon.

"Time to move, Churchy. There's a whole horde of... of... well, a whole horde of something coming along a road just over there. And I think they will be passing right by us."

"Get Nefol, Cally. Havers, we're moving out."

Three people glided quickly and quietly across the barren terrain to lie behind a small hump by the road. One other followed, hauling a large man in an awkward fashion. The man being dragged emitted grunts and expletives as they travelled.

So much for the road, thought Kirkgordon. A track was probably a better description, as only a slight wearing of the ground indicated the path. But he could hear footsteps coming. Well, he could hear something coming. There was a noise and it included multiple sounds, but not footsteps. Hiding behind the hump, Kirkgordon signalled his team to have their weapons at the ready before taking an arrow from his quiver. The markings on the feathers told him its function, and he smiled at the idea that presented itself. He recognized the sound coming. He could hear hopping.

Kirkgordon held Austerley's head to the ground so that he couldn't peer too far over the terrain and alert others to their presence. The rest of the group could be trusted and Kirkgordon flashed a *How many?* sign to Havers. *Thirty to forty* came the reply. Better not to get noticed.

Soon Kirkgordon's eyeline was dominated by humanoid figures that looked like upright frogs. They were the fully developed counterparts of those he had seen on the Scottish island, and most had lost all traces of humanity. The eyes were bloated and the legs were spindly below the knee but wide at the thigh. Webbed feet kicked up dust as they hopped. At least there must be water, thought Kirkgordon. These things couldn't survive in this dryness.

Looking at the rest of the team, Kirkgordon was not surprised to sense uneasiness in Calandra and Havers. Both had nearly lost their lives to these creatures before. Nefol was sullen-facedly staring at the parade. Several times Austerley tried to raise his head only to find it gently pushed back down by Kirkgordon, who had witnessed Austerley's negative reactions too many times. Most fire brigades would kill to have a siren like an Austerley breakdown.

The creatures were almost out of view when they suddenly stopped. One of the frog-men left the front of the party and joined a taller frog-man at the rear. There were various croaks and shakes of their heads, then a harsher croak brought the whole party around. They started to hop as one towards the hump that hid Kirkgordon and Austerley.

"Churchy!" came a hushed whisper.

"Not now, Indy!"

"But my foot, it's pounding. It's vibrating. Moving."

Kirkgordon looked down and saw the boot over Austerley's black foot rippling like a wave across its surface. His eyes widened as the foot swelled and contracted. Looking back up, he saw the frog-men hopping frantically towards their position.

"Cally! Havers! Grab Austerley and run. That way. And don't stop until you're clear of me."

His partners did not hesitate, each linking an arm under Austerley's and dragging the former professor away. Austerley was stunned at first but then he began to shout.

"My foot. It's pounding. It's pulsing. Look my foot!"

Nefol stood beside Kirkgordon with her staff at the ready, but Kirkgordon rounded on her.

"Get away, Nefol, go. Leave me. I know what I'm doing."

Looking up, Nefol saw the frog-man horde drawing closer, less than twenty metres away now. The young girl shook her head and focused on the oncoming targets.

"Nefol! Oh heck, hang on then." Kirkgordon stepped across Nefol, placing himself between the horde and the girl. She watched him draw his bow and saw the markings on the feathers. Dropping to her knees, she placed herself at Kirkgordon's heels and grabbed his legs with one hand, planting her staff into the ground with the other.

The horde was ten metres away when Kirkgordon loosed the arrow. The lead frog-man had just taken to the air with a large push from his massive thighs and the arrow sailed past him. It looked like Kirkgordon had lost this battle. The creature continued its flight and was in its downward arc, arms raised and about to land on Kirkgordon's head when the arrow pierced the ground some twenty metres away.

The frog-man felt a pull from behind, as if a lasso had reached out and grabbed his body. For a moment he was held suspended in the air, then he started to edge backwards. Kirkgordon smiled as he watched the horde being dragged into the vortex that the arrow had produced. A mighty wind blew past his shoulders and he felt Nefol clutching him tightly. He crouched in front of her to block her progress towards the vortex. One by one, the frog-men were whipped from their feet into the newly formed abyss, a howling sound accompanying their demise.

Kirkgordon knew that the vortex had no effect on the shooter, but he was also aware that everyone around him would get pulled towards it. Inside his head, a little doubt banged upon the door and asked whether his friends had gotten far enough away. After all, there was so little vegetation or solid matter to grab onto. Watching the last frog-man disappear into the blackness, he heard shouts from Austerley and Havers. The hole was closing back up but the pair raced past him like they were on invisible carts. When the vortex collapsed, Austerley was five metres in front of Kirkgordon, face down in the dirt. Havers was lying on his back, having spread himself in an attempt to slow his progress.

"I told you to cling to the staff." Turning, Kirkgordon saw Calandra with a scold on her face, her eyes pinned on Austerley. Her black wings were spread open and she gave off a regal air, looking like a Valkyrie. "Nefol, are you okay?"

The young girl nodded and released her grip on Kirkgordon. Havers stood up, glanced around, and brushed the dirt from his outfit.

"Well, I guess that was good thinking, Mr Kirkgordon, but shall we proceed?"

"In a minute, Mr Havers," Kirkgordon replied. "There are a few things to consider first." Kirkgordon turned to Nefol, who smiled back at him.

"Next time, Nefol, if I say run, then you run."

Nefol's face turned sullen. "Next time, then, kindly tell your team what you are doing." Before Kirkgordon could answer, Nefol moped off towards Calandra, who was giving Kirkgordon a mother's look of *Was that really necessary?*

"And as for you, Indy," said Kirkgordon, "what's the deal with your foot? It was like it was drawing the frog-men to it."

Austerley nodded and, although still winded, started to speak.

"Yes... I think so... We are in the Nether lands."

"Holland?" asked Calandra.

"No! The back lands. It doesn't translate well. Creatures, things here... it's like they're drawn to evil, or so I've read. I don't know how, but they know. And that damn witch was full of evil."

"Don't start that, Indy. You took the foot," scolded Kirkgordon.

As Austerley snarled at Kirkgordon, Havers suggested a solution.

"Well, this would appear to be an unnecessary risk. I suggest removal of the appendage."

"How?" asked Kirkgordon.

"What do you mean, how? No one's taking my foot off!"

"Shush, Indy. How, Havers?"

"I have a blade, Mr Kirkgordon, and you know I can handle a blade."

"Churchy, you keep that lunatic off me. Havers, you've been psycho since the priest got burnt. No one's taking my foot off me."

"Indy, not in front of her," raged Calandra as Nefol stormed off.

"Bloody magic, Indy," spat Kirkgordon. "Five minutes in and you guys are at each other."

"Well, shall I?" asked Havers.

"No!" shouted Austerley.

"No. Not yet, Mr Havers. We are in the clear at the moment," answered Kirkgordon.

"But for how long?"

"Long enough. But I'll bear your suggestion in mind."

"No you bloody won't," interjected Austerley.

"Enough!" Kirkgordon looked for Calandra and found her a little distance away. "Give Austerley a hand, will you?" he called to her. "And then we'd better get moving."

"Okay, Indy, but where?"

"Austerley, you know where we are, but do you know it exactly?" asked Kirkgordon.

"No, nothing except that this is the Nether... back lands."

"Well, the frog-men came from down that way, so there must be something there," said Kirkgordon. "Let's find out what it is."

The Fog

"Austerley's slowing us down, Cally."

"Well, you can hardly leave him behind, can you?" replied Calandra, removing her leather jacket and tying it round her waist. She caught Kirkgordon's eyes flashing across her torso and his appreciative inhalation of breath. The black crop top had been chosen for its freedom, keeping her limbs clear of any snagging clothing in a fight. But yes, she admitted to herself, also because it always makes him look.

"No, I can't. But dammit, this pace is so slow. How far do you think we've covered?"

"Five miles, tops."

"Exactly. I even put Havers with him to see if that would get Austerley's arse into gear, but he seems to be dragging the foot."

"You weren't seriously considering Havers' proposal, were you? It's pretty barbaric, hacking someone's foot off."

"If there are hordes after us because of it then yes, I will consider it." Kirkgordon looked away from Calandra's frown. "I know he means a lot to you, but that foot could get us all killed. Havers does have a point."

"Yes, and Havers has an agenda too, Churchy. And his agenda is not the same as yours, be sure of that. I've known him a long time and I've never seen him this moody. There's only one thing he wants and that's Farthington's head on a plate. He'll sacrifice Alana for that, trust me. And he'll push Nefol that way too."

Kirkgordon watched the young girl up ahead. There was a resolve about her but it was born from determination, not hate. Kirkgordon was used to protecting one person, one VIP. Now he had a team to balance and understand.

"It's starting to get properly dark," said Calandra. "We should find somewhere to lie low. Somewhere with shelter and some walls. I don't fancy taking on anything in the dark round here."

Kirkgordon called Nefol back and told her to go and scout ahead for some shelter. The good news of a building within sight was soon returned and the party made a beeline for it. The path had been monotonous, the landscape a constant plain of dark soil and pathetic outcrops of failing plant growth, but now there was a haven to lift everyone's spirits and the pace quickened towards it.

Kirkgordon halted the party a little short of the building. He realized this left them in the open, but as anyone inside would have seen them coming from a good distance away, he felt it didn't compromise the party any further. The building was wooden in construction and appeared to be a barn with some high windows and a large double door on one side. Rotting timbers could be seen and there were open holes where the perishing was at its greatest.

Nefol and Calandra were sent to check first around and then inside the building. A few minutes later Calandra's head popped out one of the high windows and called the men forward.

Stepping inside, Kirkgordon surveyed what appeared to be

an empty barn. There was a central ladder leading to a high loft but otherwise the bottom floor was entirely empty. The same soil they had trudged over also covered the lower area. Calandra shouted down from above and Kirkgordon climbed the ladder to the upper part. There were large plant leaves piled up at one end. Quite rounded for a leaf, each dark-green piece was at least the height of a man. Wondering where in this land the leaves could have come from, Kirkgordon touched one and felt its coarse skin.

"Bit weird, eh?" said Calandra.

"I know. Why are these here? But it's gone very dark outside, Cally, and I guess it's going to have to do. Let's crack a couple of glow sticks and see what's to eat from the packs."

In order to keep their speed up, Kirkgordon had rejected the idea of bringing any large provisions with them and had opted for some special high-energy bars and a couple of canteens. After Havers had helped a moaning Austerley up the ladder, the party settled down to their meagre rations. When dinner was concluded, Kirkgordon suggested a roster to keep watch through the night. The roster included everyone except Austerley, who was deemed to be as much use on guard duty as a sloth.

Kirkgordon shut his eyes, wrapped himself in one of the leaves and struggled to get comfortable before falling asleep. Dank soil appeared swirling in his dreams. He located his feet stuck in a rotting bog beneath him. He felt his arms being pulled in opposite directions and looked first to his right where he saw Alana, his wife, hauling at his limb. She was sweating profusely but Kirkgordon was sure that underwear, and in particular that rather thin variety she was wearing, wasn't really outdoor attire. Although a strange image, it wasn't unpleasant, and he had to force himself to look at what was pulling his other arm.

His jaw dropped as he recognized the pale skin and dark hair. Calandra stood there in her crop top and little else, pulling his arm, the exertion showing on her face. Due to the nature of her cold skin she sweated only a little, but her expression was similar to Alana's. His head swung to and fro from one woman to the other, more and more rapidly. Eventually they started to move together until they were in front of him and were holding hands. They had stopped fighting over him and were now drawing him towards them in a joint effort. Wow, thought Kirkgordon, I didn't see this coming.

Cold flooded both cheeks. His eyes flung open and he stared into Calandra's face.

"Hey, sunshine, up you get. My turn for a rest." He watched her face turn from a smile to a quizzical look. "Are you okay, Churchy?"

"Fine, Cally. Just fine. Only a dream."

"Really. What about?"

"Nothing."

"Had some effect for nothing, you were moaning names and smiling a lot." Calandra grinned at Kirkgordon's awkwardness. "Nothing dodgy I hope."

"Nah, nothing dodgy."

She dropped her jeans and rolled herself into a leaf. "But I guess the crop top's a winner." And with that she turned her head away, closing the conversation.

It's not fair, thought Kirkgordon. A man only ever needs one good woman. Why is there a choice? Couldn't fate just make them turn up at different times in your lives? Or for a reincarnation? Walking to the window, a thought struck him.

Choice. When did it ever become a choice?

Kirkgordon stared off into the blackness, the night sky covered, and watched a mist slowly form in the immediate vicinity. A shiver ran down his spine. The air was dry, making him question where the mist had come from. But who was to know how the environment of a place like this worked? Surely natural laws could be suspended, or maybe even a different nature operate. A few years ago he wouldn't have credited a place like this could exist, or any of the creatures he had seen. Heck, he never thought any woman could challenge his love for Alana, never mind an eight-hundred-year-old cursed ice babe. Babe? Too cheesy for such a beauty.

A tap on the shoulder broke his train of thought. Austerley was standing with a worried look on his face.

"Churchy," the former professor whispered, "would you let him do it?"

"Do what?" Kirkgordon knew what was coming but he had to delay the moment.

"My foot. Would you let Havers take my foot off?"

The hands were trembling. Kirkgordon had seen real fear in Austerley's eyes before and recognized the terror.

"I can't take it again. Whatever you think, however much you hate me for getting this foot, you can't take it off me. Havers is a cold bastard and he'll do it. He told me, over and over again on the way here. You know I can't stop him. He's too quick for me." Austerley looked down at the cause of his troubles. He had removed his shoes to sleep and was barefooted. The black foot had a sheen to it and he could see his own face reflected. "Farthington took my other foot. Don't let Havers take this one."

"What's in it, Indy?" Kirkgordon spoke softly. "Can it be

healed?"

"I think so. I have heard of those who can." Austerley's voice was unconvincing.

"Why can't you? You swapped the feet in the first place."

"Yes, but it wanted to come to me. You can't just take an appendage, it has to want to come to you. It must feel purpose. It must have felt a better future with me."

Kirkgordon was confused. When Austerley spoke about these mysterious chants and places, there was a part of Kirkgordon that just wanted to switch off and denounce it all as mumbo-jumbo. But the mumbo-jumbo had grown a physical form and tried to kill him on too many occasions for him to dismiss it. So Kirkgordon faced the demons head-on with a brutal logic that he hoped kept him sane. But now he heard the twang of the elastic snapping inside his head, as logic began to break down in the face of a highly polished ebony foot.

"You're in the stadium and I'm stuck in the car park on this one, Indy. Your foot, or rather Tania's foot as it was before it migrated to you, made a decision to come to you?" Austerley nodded. "All that chanting and stuff you were doing at the time was just some sort of coaxing? So what did you say? You can learn tap with me? You should see my rumba? I mean, what could a foot want? Hey, get on the end of my leg, I'm the new Kevin Bacon. Kick off your Sunday shoes—"

"Stop it. Don't mention that name."

"What?"

"Too many dreams. He's in too many dreams. Wretched film."

Kirkgordon reined in his mockery. I need this guy. For all the hell he's brought upon me, I need this guy. But hold on. Why would the foot jump over? I mean, look at this wretch. Why would the foot want to be on him? I always thought it was just Indy taking it, but now it seems it came willingly. How do you find purpose as a foot?

Austerley was gazing at the floor. His shoulders were slumped and Kirkgordon thought he detected some measure of contriteness. *He's almost a sinner in prayer.* Kirkgordon reached out a hand and placed it on Austerley's shoulder.

"I'll not let him cut it off unless it's absolutely essential. But you need to find us one of these healers. And soon. That foot's already brought us the frog-men. We're out of our depth already, Indy. And you need to find Alana."

"I will. We can't have Farthington hunting us forever. That son of a bitch Havers is right enough. We need Farthington dead."

"No, Indy. We need Alana back and our arses residing in the real world again."

"But this is real, Churchy. You know that, don't you?"

"I know very little, Indy, just this: the day you took me down that grave in New England was the day my life went to hell. All I want is to get it back."

The two men stared out the window, allowing all mention of the graveyard occurrence to disappear into the darkness. Kirkgordon breathed easily, assuming the motionless stance of a sentry, listening into the blackness. But soon he could hear Austerley's breathing deepen. At first it was like a gymnast inhaling deeply before the apparatus, but soon it became a swimmer gasping for breath. Turning round, Kirkgordon saw Austerley's face in terror, sweating profusely from the palest skin. His right arm was outstretched and his digit finger pointed out of the window.

"What the hell's the matter?"

"There!" answered Austerley.

"What?"

"The fog."

"Yes, it's fog. Unusual and that, but hey, this is the Nether world or whatever you're calling it. So what's the problem?"

"That," said Austerley, "is not fog! The book" – Austerley spoke some unintelligible sounds – "from the Fandomis library, it mentions that. Not fog. Too dry here for fog. But they travel as fog."

"Who are they?"

Another unintelligible word. "Blood sprites. Something like that in English."

"Are they dangerous?"

"Like a land piranha. They'll strip us to the bone."

"How?" Kirkgordon was getting agitated. "How, Indy? Do they attack as a fog?"

"No, if only. Oh God, if only."

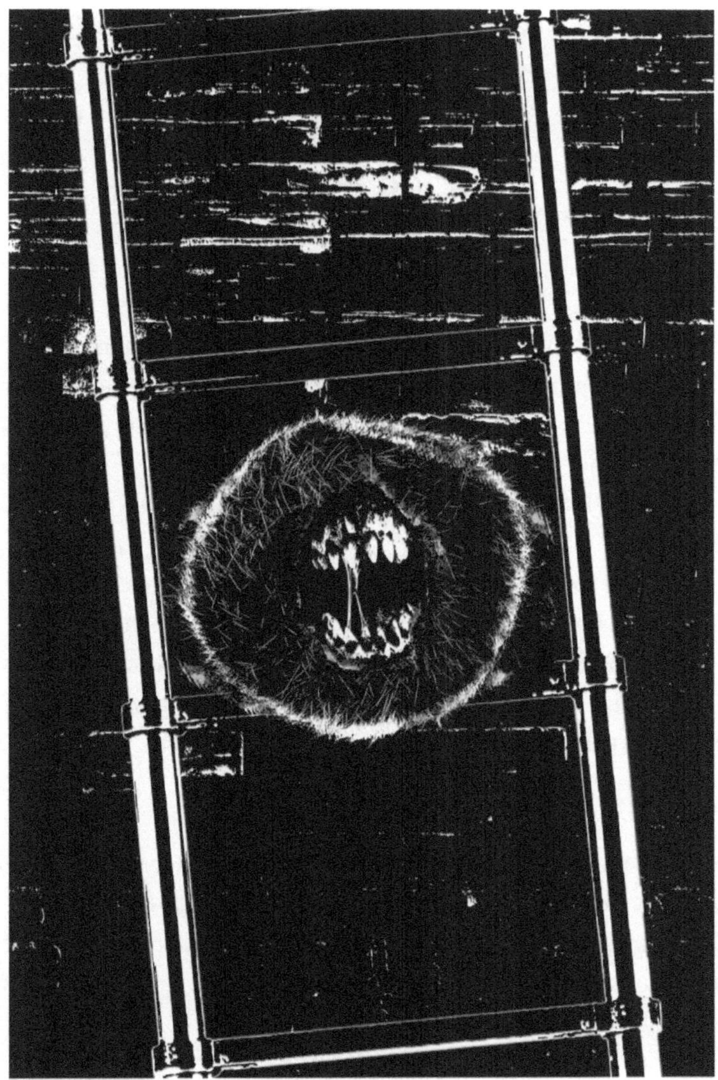

Blood Sprites

Kirkgordon pulled apart the leaf covering Calandra and roughly grabbed her shoulder. His eyes fixed on her face, ignoring her pale legs and tight torso. Now was not the time.

"Hey!" shouted Calandra, grabbing Kirkgordon's wrist and twisting it.

"Ah! Get off, Cally. And get up. Indy says we have company. Keep it quiet." Kirkgordon moved swiftly to Nefol and Havers, waking them up in turn. By the time he had turned back towards Calandra, she had dressed in her jeans and leather jacket and held her trusty staff in one hand.

What is it? mouthed Calandra.

Blood sprites, came the silent reply. Kirkgordon shrugged his shoulders at her questioning look. Austerley was providing credence to the belief that blood sprites could be dangerous as he sat on the floor head in hands, shaking. Bloody hell, thought Kirkgordon, the least he could do was tell us what these things are before he goes loco.

Nefol was at the window peering gingerly outside.

"What are we expecting?" she asked.

"Blood sprites, according to Austerley," answered Kirkgordon, his voice hushed. "No, I don't know what they are either, but they are out there in some sort of fog."

"Fog. I don't see any fog."

Kirkgordon peered past the girl. The fog was gone. Oh heck, they must be on the move. Turning to his group, he gestured at Calandra to widen out. His eyes sought Havers for a similar instruction but the government man was holding Austerley's hands and relentlessly whispering a question at him.

"Havers!" Kirkgordon urged under his breath. There was no reaction so Kirkgordon raised his voice slightly louder.

"Havers. Flank out."

Standing quickly, Havers strode past Kirkgordon. "They are flesh beings. Mr Austerley confirms this, so they should be easier to dispatch than most of the Dillingham unseemlies." Havers grinned and dropped some glow sticks over the side of the loft area, lighting up the ground floor. He pulled two handguns from his garment.

"I said no guns."

"I fail to see why not. Damned rude to deny a fellow his tools of the trade."

"Havers, you know why. You damn well know."

There was a thudding at the large barn doors. Kirkgordon spun round and saw the fixtures on the large wooden panels straining. Look at the pressure on those, he thought. These doors won't last long. They must have some big buggers amongst them.

"Everyone ready!" called Kirkgordon. "Remember, the bigger they are, the harder they fall."

The doors collapsed inward, splintering into pieces as they hit the ground. Scrambling across the top of the failed gates were dozens of small furballs, like a dark sea. The little creatures spread out round the room, tumbling over one another, with loud hungry rasps coming from the pack.

"Havers, drop the ladder!"

Taking Kirkgordon's suggestion on board, Havers ran to the ladder but was met by a furball which had scaled its height in no time. Drawing his pistol, Havers ignored the pair of large fangs which emerged from a mouth deep inside the creature. Two shots rang out. Havers hit the furball both times and it dropped off the ladder. Any further climbers were dispatched as Havers kicked the ladder clear.

"No! Shuggoth! Mother Hydra." Austerley was on his feet, wildly lashing out around him. "Markings on the wall. No, Churchy. On the wall. Seal it. Seal the hole, or they'll come."

Kirkgordon tried to grab Austerley but he was caught by a flailing arm which momentarily sent him spinning. No, thought Kirkgordon, not now. I can't deal with him like this. Turning back towards Austerley, Kirkgordon barrelled into the large professor, knocking him to the ground, then swiftly struck him in the neck, silencing him. Austerley's eyes shut and he went limp.

"Nefol, stand over him. Let nothing touch him."

As Nefol reacted, Calandra called, "Churchy, they're climbing the walls. They're coming." Havers started dispatching little furballs as they leapt from the walls onto the upstairs platform. Each shot was right on target and repeated with a speed that defied belief. Kirkgordon pulled an arrow from his quiver and shot it into the floor. The familiar face of a giant holding a hammer greeted him and Kirkgordon pointed at the furballs.

"Don't waste your arrows," yelled Nefol, "they are flesh." I can do nothing right in the eyes of that girl, thought Kirkgordon. But then he then saw why as his giant was bitten by one furball. This slowed the large creature and he was soon engulfed.

"Mr Kirkgordon, if you have any suggestions, now would be a good time. I think we shall be overrun by these little blighters within a few minutes. As soon as I dispatch them, more keep coming. Maybe one of your excellent vortices is required."

"It'll suck in everyone, Havers. I'll be the only one standing."

"Well, I was going to suggest using Mr Austerley, but as you have knocked him out, I guess you're not keen on his solutions."

That's it, Havers, take the piss, why don't you? thought Kirkgordon. But he's right. We have no exit. I doubt we can fight through them all. This needs an Austerley solution. Kirkgordon looked at the lump on the floor that was Austerley. Yeah, I can lift him.

"Cally, can you hold them here for a minute? You and Nefol?"

"A minute's about it," shouted Calandra as she swatted the furballs away with lightning speed. Kirkgordon nodded.

"Havers, get me a hole in the roof and get through it." Nefol took over from Havers at keeping the furballs back. Havers quickly shot the roof away above him. Grabbing some of the leaves, he piled them on top of one another and was able to raise himself high enough to jump and grab on to the roof. He pulled himself through the gap then turned around and poked his head back through. Seeing Nefol in trouble, Havers blew several furballs away with another burst of gunfire.

Kirkgordon had thrown Austerley over his shoulder and was climbing the pile of leaves. At the top, he readjusted Austerley so that he was holding the professor by the hips. Quickly, he threw him up with all his strength and saw Havers wrap an arm around Austerley's neck and drag him through the gap. His eyes fixed above him, Kirkgordon felt his feet go from under him as the pile of leaves slid off one another and he tumbled to the floor.

Calandra was over the top of him, batting away the creatures as he recovered.

"I'm going to the roof to wake Austerley. Let's hope he's got something. Hold as long as you can!"

Calandra didn't even acknowledge as she strode back into the mass of furballs, her staff moving at blinding speed. The edges were white hot and Kirkgordon was stunned by her courage once again. As he regathered the leaf pile, he noticed the same courage in Nefol as the girl tore into the seething mass before her.

Kirkgordon threw his arms up through the gap, ready to reach out for the edges, but something grabbed him and he was unceremoniously hauled through the gap. He tumbled onto the roof and rolled to regain his feet.

"Mr Kirkgordon, kindly get our oaf awake. There isn't much time." With that, Havers leaned back into the hole in the roof and started dispatching more rounds into the horde of furballs. Kirkgordon turned to the motionless Austerley on the floor and picked his head up by the hair.

"Wake up, Indy," yelled Kirkgordon as he slapped his colleague across the face repeatedly. Austerley did not stir and Kirkgordon increased the intensity of his strike. Dammit, Indy, wake up. For once we actually need you, so damn well wake up.

"Mr Kirkgordon, where is our illustrious professor? I'm going to need to extract the ladies as they are getting overrun. We need him now, Mr Kirkgordon!"

Dammit, Havers, like I don't know that. But this beast just isn't waking.

From the corner of his eye, Kirkgordon saw Calandra emerge

through the hole in the roof. She was bleeding from her torso and screaming back into the hole.

"Nefol, get out! Now! Don't you dare stay. Out now."

Austerley was starting to murmur but his eyes were still firmly shut. Heck, they needed to buy some time.

"Cally," said Kirkgordon, "go to the far corner and spin that staff. See if you can set the building on fire. Knock something off the edge to cover the exit. Get that on fire first."

Calandra turned to Havers and screamed at him to get Nefol out before racing to the edge of the building where she began to spin her staff. With her feet rooted, the weapon became a blur and white-hot edges formed. Calandra screamed loudly as she struggled to hold on to the spinning staff before abruptly slamming it into the roof edge. The wood buckled under the strike and ignited. Flames quickly spread and Calandra thumped her staff into the heat. The edge of the roof gave way and fell ablaze across the open exit where the barn doors had been.

Havers was pulling Nefol out of the hole in the roof. Screaming in pain, she pointed at Kirkgordon. Hell, kid, I know, but the stupid bugger won't wake up. Come on, Austerley! Kirkgordon had Austerley by the shoulders now and was shaking him hard. Austerley's head rocked to and fro violently and he began to stir.

"The little creatures are becoming quite affected by the fire, Mr Kirkgordon. I suggest you wake up our friend by any means possible. Your inferno is driving them all towards the hole in quite a frenzied fashion."

How does Havers stay so damn cool? Come on, Indy. Come on.

Austerley's eyes opened. He stared straight ahead at Kirkgordon and started to sniff the air.

"Churchy, do I smell burning?"

"Burning? I'll burn your arse if you don't get something going. We're on a roof, the building's on fire. The furballs are coming up a hole to eat us. We need off this roof now. We need those furballs put down."

"Furballs?" asked Austerley.

"Blood sprites. The fog things."

"Oh. Well, I could..."

After a period of kicking the furballs back into the barn, Havers had retreated to open up on the creatures from a distance. The shots rang out into the dark, each one precise and taking a casualty. Austerley jumped at the sound.

"Shuggoth! Mother Hydra. On the walls, Churchy, on the walls! Close it, close it."

Oh hell. Kirkgordon tried to grab Austerley but he turned wild again, thrashing around. Calandra looked across from where she had run to help Nefol. The girl was lying on the ground but still pointing at Kirkgordon.

"Churchy, she's been bitten. There's a large chunk out of her thigh. We need to go!"

"And I feel our exit cannot be too soon, Mr Kirkgordon." There was just a tremor in Havers' voice.

How? thought Kirkgordon. How do I get off this roof, if not by jumping? It's too far; we'd break our legs at best. Nefol was still pointing at Kirkgordon and he knelt down beside her. "Sorry. You shouldn't be here. I've wronged your father."

"Kirkgordon..." Her breath was rasping. "Shut... up... The arrow... green... red... feathers."

"What's she saying?" asked Calandra, who was now standing between Nefol and the hole, fighting back the occasional furball who had beaten Havers' guns.

Kirkgordon didn't wait. He dived into his quiver and located the arrow Nefol had mentioned. Drawing his bow, he took aim into the hole in the roof.

"No..." said Nefol weakly.

Kirkgordon aimed. Just as he was about to release, he felt a tap on his leg. Looking down, he saw Nefol pointing off into the distance. And then she closed her eyes.

"Now, Mr Kirkgordon! They are coming through!"

Kirkgordon fired the arrow into the distance. As the projectile was loosed from his bow, a rope began to form along its flight path, holding an impossible curve. Once the arrow had hit the ground the rope remained and Kirkgordon grabbed it. He pulled it tight and was surprised that when he let go, it remained in its supported form.

"Time to go, Mr Kirkgordon. Been a while since the old death slide." Havers grabbed at the rope but his hands fell right through it. "Ah, slight problem, old bean. I think that it's only solid when the shooter touches it."

Kirkgordon saw the furballs pouring through the hole and Calandra grabbed Nefol off the floor. The building was now burning intensely and part of the roof over the original exit had collapsed completely.

"We go. Grab a leg or get burnt!" Kirkgordon threw his quiver strap over the rope and began to run. Glancing round, he saw Calandra racing behind him with Nefol on her shoulder. Havers had Austerley by the scruff of the neck. Kirkgordon jumped and let his arms take the strain as he dangled from the rope. Within a second, two arms had wrapped themselves round his legs and, like an amateur acrobatic team, they began the slide to freedom.

The Cliff

Kirkgordon grimaced in pain. He had wrapped the leather strap of the quiver around his wrists as he jumped. His left hand had let go in agony at the weight of Havers and Austerley jumping onto his left side and all that remained was the strap cutting into his wrist. Glancing to his right, he saw Calandra with one arm wrapped around his leg and her other arm pulling Nefol close to her chest, anchored under the child's armpits. Calandra's ponytail was gone and her hair was blowing out loosely behind her. Now that's a sight to die to, thought Kirkgordon.

A crash behind him made him turn his head. The barn was now fully ablaze and collapsing. Strange howls were coming from within and the roof had sunk inward, leaving the bizarre arrow-rope hanging in space. Looking ahead of him once again, he saw the blur of darkness. Somewhere the ground was rushing up hard to meet him, but the light of the fire had blinded his eyes too much and the distance to the ground below was a mystery.

Calandra dropped first. She stumbled as her burden caused her to lose footing and she crashed to the ground. She tried to wrap herself around Nefol but ended up burying her own head, face first, into the dusty soil with Nefol lying beneath her.

Havers dropped Austerley and the professor crashed spectacularly into the dust, ending up in a heap. Then Havers alighted, touching down lightly onto his feet. With his load dispersed, Kirkgordon lifted his legs out of the way in time to feel the smack of his arse hitting the ground. For a moment he continued to hold onto the rope above. Then, looking up to free his hands, he saw it was gone.

"Everyone okay?" was Kirkgordon's optimistic cry.

"Nefol's not good, Churchy," said Calandra. "She's lost blood and is pretty banged up. And she's been bitten by those things. Look!"

Kirkgordon ran over and saw the glow from Nefol's leg where she had been bitten several times.

"We need to take her back home," said Calandra.

"There's no time, Miss Calandra. Farthington is our objective. Unless we can find something to help her on our way then she's an unfortunate casualty."

"Casualty! I'll break you apart if you abandon her, Havers."

Kirkgordon looked round at Austerley but the occult genius was silent and obviously out cold. Damn it, that stupid arse might actually know something about these bites. "Havers, have you ever seen bites like these?"

Havers shook his head.

"You, Calandra?" Another negative. "Well then, Havers is right."

Calandra threw a shocked look at Kirkgordon. "I'll take her back alone if I have to." Little icicles were forming at her tear ducts. "She damn well saved your life, Churchy."

"I know, Cally. But listen. Who knows what that wound will do? I don't. None of us do. I doubt all Havers' resources back home could manage it. And with Indy gone to sleep then we need another expert. The frog-men came from somewhere,

Cally. That's a somewhere which just might have help. It's a long shot but it's all I've got. So we need to continue, but at a pace."

"And what about Mr Austerley? How do you expect us to move his rather considerable hide onward? I barely hung onto him during our descent," said Havers.

"I'll take him, Havers. You take Nefol. And Cally, you go out front, keep the way clear."

"I'm not letting him take her, Churchy. He's likely to dump her somewhere as a *casualty*. I'll guard her."

"No, Cally, you won't. You're faster than us, you've got wings to get up in the air and look ahead, and you're the best fighter. I need you up front. Don't worry, I'll gut Havers if he does anything to harm that child."

Calandra nodded and gave a thin smile. Then she turned around and raced off into the dark.

"Gut me, Mr Kirkgordon? How very crude," sneered Havers.

"Trust me, it won't be a clean cut. Now let's go." Kirkgordon grabbed Austerley by the shoulders and sat him upright. Then he heaved Austerley by his stomach onto the opposite shoulder from his bow. *Crap, he is heavy.*

It wasn't so much a jog as a fast walk, but with Austerley's weight bearing down on him, Kirkgordon reckoned his progress was impressive. Calandra routed to and fro making sure the way was clear and that their direction led back to the path the frog-men had been on. Occasionally Kirkgordon would see her rise up on her wings, scanning into the distance. He found his eyes wandering along her back and then down her legs from her trim rear. He put this down to a momentary lapse, but he knew in his heart that Cally was growing into the place Alana had always occupied.

Havers was keeping good pace but it surprised Kirkgordon that the Major wasn't trying to pull ahead and drive them on. The wounds Farthington had given him must still be affecting him.

"Where the hell am I?" Austerley's voice. So he's waking up, thought Kirkgordon.

"On the run with me again, Indy. And when we get back, you are going on a diet," said Kirkgordon. He believed that humour in adversity was always uplifting, although that maxim was certainly being put to the test.

"What happened to her?" Austerley nodded in Nefol's direction.

"She saved our arses, Indy. But she got some bites from those furballs."

Austerley made the strange sound he had made when he had seen the fog. "That's their name, actually. Is it glowing?"

"Yes."

"Poor kid. She's infected. The creatures replicate by planting eggs from their mouths into victims. They bury in and you need some" – another strange sound came out – "to remove them."

"So where do you get this stuff? What does it look like?"

"I don't know. The book was a general travel guide in the language of another dimension. I didn't really understand everything. We'll need to find someone. A healer. Head for where the frog-men came from."

"Already ahead of you, my overweight friend."

"Makes a change," said Austerley and closed his eyes. Kirkgordon was stunned to hear snoring some five minutes later.

The night turned into a damp and cold day before Calandra returned from one of her scouting missions with news.

"There's something up ahead. This whole plain ends at an

enormous cliff face as wide as I can see. At the bottom of the cliff there's dense forest, and within that forest there's a city rising up. It's truly massive and it appears to have links coming away from it."

"Is there any way down the cliff?" asked Kirkgordon.

"Yes, there's a fairly wide path, enough for carts. It'll be very open but it seems to be the only way down."

"Well, that's a risk we're going to have to take. Nefol hasn't said a word. Havers tightened up the wound with part of his outfit and the bleeding's stopped, but she's still unconscious," said Kirkgordon.

Austerley made one of his unintelligible sounds. "That's what it's called. The City in the Shadow."

"Shadow of what?" asked Kirkgordon.

"I don't know, but it was definitely *in the shadow* rather than *in shadow*."

"And you are sure of that? It's not like you're always one hundred percent accurate."

"You try and read" – another unintelligible noise – "and it's my thirty-seventh language by the way. I doubt you can even read French."

"Enough!" said Calandra. "She needs help. Can we get a move on? In fact, why don't I run on ahead with her. I'll get there quicker."

"And do what, Miss Calandra?" interrupted Havers. "You can't speak the language, you can't read anything. How would you find help? I fear you require the services of Mr Austerley."

"No, Cally, we stick together," said Kirkgordon. "But let's step up the pace, Havers."

"I wasn't aware I was the one holding us back, dear fellow."

No, thought Kirkgordon, it's been me carrying Austerley. But in fairness I do have the heaviest weight. "Okay, Cally, lead the way."

Another hour brought them to the cliff edge. As Kirkgordon looked around the vast plain behind him, he saw no one. Turning to look at the forest below, through the trees he saw roads busy with traffic. And dominating it all was the city.

At the centre were enormous spires reaching up towards the sky, reminding Kirkgordon of a sci-fi movie. The architecture was crisp and clean and every piece of stone was jet black. Outside of these central pieces the city seemed positively medieval, with all buildings being wooden in construction. They spread out from the central core, gradually diminishing in height until there was an outer circle of ramshackle huts and collapsed houses. There appeared to be major routes running through the city, and even from the cliff edge the noise and bustle could be heard.

The path down from the plain cut back and forward into the cliff face and had clearly been designed rather than created by the impact of time. Descending the very steep slopes, Kirkgordon found his knees screaming at him as he fought to keep Austerley on his shoulder, which was numb from the constant carrying and jolting. With no feeling in the shoulder with which to balance Austerley, Kirkgordon found himself hanging on harder.

Halfway down the slope, the path twisted out from the cliff face to give a glorious view of the rock itself. Kirkgordon was astonished to see a building cut into the cliff face.

"Damn, that must have been a lot of work. You could nearly fit an army into that," said Austerley.

"And you don't know how far back it goes, either," added Calandra.

"I think you'll find the word is 'cyclopean', Mr Kirkgordon," said Havers. "Some of the room sizes would appear to be on a scale with some great works found in Antarctica. But I don't see any symbols or markings on the outside indicating who the construction belongs to."

"And frankly, guys, I don't care. Nefol needs help, so let's move," insisted Calandra.

It was another three hours before they reached the bottom of the slope and found a road leading into the dense forest. The air was dank and most of the trees were rotting. There was little green foliage but the light was kept out by the sheer number of branches emerging from each tree, like an ad hoc wicker canopy. The path weaved round thicker patches of trees, clearly constructed by a determined mind, for the density of trees was becoming claustrophobic.

As they turned round a tight bend, the party was confronted by a small party of roughly clad soldiers. Each was wearing leather garments and a metallic hat, accompanied by a small weapon at the soldier's side. Maces, hammers, clubs. Looks like a local militia of some sort, thought Kirkgordon.

On seeing Kirkgordon's party, one of the soldiers starting yelling instructions at them. When it was clear there was no hint of comprehension, he shouted other words in a different language. And then a third language.

"Austerley, are you getting any of these?" asked Kirkgordon.

"All of them. They are pretty common languages, just not on earth."

"But it's not the Nether Land language. The one you read."

"That's old, Churchy, very old. I doubt many people would speak or even read it today. Maybe those of a religious bent."

"Well," said Kirkgordon, setting Austerley on his feet, "go

and sort our passage out."

While the rest of the group held back and huddled around Nefol, Austerley hobbled up to the militia and began to converse at a rapid rate. There were shouts and laughs from the soldiers while Austerley held a sorry form, hunched over and slightly off kilter, leaning on his smaller foot. Eventually he trudged back to the group.

"They want money to let us pass. They say they are the city militia and have the right to take road taxes. So if we want past, we have to pay."

"Did you tell them we have no money?" asked Calandra. "And that we have a girl in need?"

"He didn't mention the money, which was quite wise, Mr Austerley, but he did tell them of Nefol's plight," said Havers. Kirkgordon looked quizzically at the agent. "It's a common enough language, Mr Kirkgordon."

"I guess we'll have to find something to barter with," suggested Austerley.

"Like hell," swore Calandra, her wings erupting from her back and her staff clutched in both hands. "I don't have time for this."

The City in the Shadow

"Cally, no!" implored Kirkgordon.

"It is not advisable, Mr Kirkgordon," said Havers, "to shout out your colleague's name just as she is about to attack the local authorities."

Calandra strode forward directly to the man who had been talking with Austerley. The man stood up to his full height and called out to his men, who took up defensive postures around their captain. Calandra began to spin her staff, but at a noticeably slower speed than when she was in full flow. Then Havers gave a simple shout.

"Guns!"

Kirkgordon saw the soldiers draw guns from their clothing and heard gunfire from beside his head. Three of the soldiers catapulted backwards into the air. The two closest to their captain were dropped by a whirl of Calandra's staff before she grabbed the captain by the throat and held him high. The rest of the guard froze on seeing their captain compromised, and for a split second there was a silence, before—

"Shuggoth! The walls, it's on the walls, Churchy. Mother Hydra! In the dark. Close it, clo—"

There was a dull thud as Austerley fell limp to the ground.

"For the last time, would you stop using the damn guns? You know it freaks the poor sod out. Was there really any need,

Havers?"

"Indeed there was, my good fellow. The opposition were drawing their own guns and I believe Miss Calandra's life, if not indeed all our lives, was in peril."

"I've seen her take out multiple Nightgaunts, Havers, so don't give me the 'she wasn't capable of handling it' speech."

"Well, Mr Kirkgordon, I'm glad you have such faith..."

"Guys, shut it!" yelled Calandra. "And Havers, tell this man I'm holding that if his men don't drop all their weapons and let us through, I am going to break his scrawny neck. We need to get moving."

Havers spoke briefly in the foreign language for some thirty seconds. After a harsh command from their leader, the militia dropped their weapons and stepped aside from the path.

"Good," said Calandra, dropping the captain. "Now somebody grab Austerley and we can get going."

"Look, forgive me for asking," said Kirkgordon, "but is anyone else here bothered we just blew away three soldiers, in full view of their cohorts, all belonging to the city we're about to go into?"

"Hardly, Mr Kirkgordon, all we did was give them a little bloody nose."

"Bloody nose, Havers? You damn well killed three of them."

"Now that would have been most foolish, my dear fellow. They were just hit with thumpers. Knocked them down like skittles. Bit of a bruise but nothing permanent. Really, Mr Kirkgordon, you do sometimes mistake me for an amateur."

"Come on," said Calandra, "every second we waste could be fatal to Nefol."

Calandra raced off ahead on the path, followed by Havers with Nefol over his shoulder. Kirkgordon slung Austerley over his back again with a curse and trudged past the bewildered militia. He gave a simple salute as he passed the captain.

"No hard feelings, guys. They were only thumpers." The look from the captain indicated that "thumpers" weren't that much of a soft touch.

Austerley came round some ten minutes later and Kirkgordon set him down then matched his pace. Havers was up ahead, out of earshot, and Calandra kept appearing in the distance signalling the all clear. Time to pick the brains of my expert, thought Kirkgordon.

"Indy, did you notice something back there?"

"What do you mean?"

"The guns, did you notice the guns?"

"Did I notice the guns? Of course I noticed the guns. Did you miss the screaming nightmare I turned into?"

"No. I meant the type. Did you see the type of gun, Indy?"

"I don't look too closely. You know I don't get on with them since the incident at the grave."

No, you don't, thought Kirkgordon. "They were Russian, Indy. That seem a bit of a coincidence?"

"Never mind that. I've been over to a few places this side and I have never seen a gun. Most of the weapons here are blades or blunt force. Rarely do you get our things over here. After all, there's a fair few creatures they won't affect."

"And the militia were human too."

"Not all, Churchy."

Kirkgordon raised his eyebrows. "Not all?"

"No. I saw a few werewolves there, one vampire certainly, though not much of a specimen, and definitely a few early stage ghouls. But I think the captain was human. In fact, when he spoke, did you not hear his accent?"

"You got an accent out of that language, Indy?"

"Oh yes," nodded Austerley vehemently. "Not just an accent, but one I can place, too. In fairness to you, it was faint, and when it comes to languages you are a bit thick."

"Never mind that. Where was it from?"

"Moscow. Definitely Moscow and probably to the north of the city. So we are on the right lines to find Farthington."

"Forgive me, Indy, but even Mr Thick here got that one. Did you notice something else?" Kirkgordon raised his eyebrows and stopped walking.

"He's got connections here. He has somehow tapped into the authorities. Selling guns to them. And it must have been a hell of a story to flog them that rubbish. Like I said, it wouldn't work on most creatures here."

"And so, when we get to the city..."

"He'll have contacts in high places. We'll be watched. Even targeted."

Kirkgordon nodded. "Look, Indy, you're an awkward bastard but I'll tell you now that if you and I don't stick together in this one we won't be coming back. Cally's got her hands full with Nefol and I'm going to let her stay with the girl and keep her safe. That means there's only you, me and Havers to cover each other, and I don't trust him one bit."

"He only has eyes on Farthington. I'd like to see that dragon in pieces too, Churchy, but I'm not dumb enough to hunt him down. If it wasn't for your Alana being here I'd not be around. I have enough problems with this damn black foot." Austerley saw Kirkgordon's lips begin to move. "And before you start, I know it was my own fault."

"No, that isn't what I was going to say." Kirkgordon caught the surprise in Austerley's face. "There's something I don't understand about your foot. When the frog-men went past it went crazy. But with the furballs and the militia, nothing. How does that work?"

"I've been thinking about that too. It never reacted to Farthington either, back in Dillingham. I think it is because it has a certain kind of darkness."

"But if it reacted to the frog-men then that means..."

"Elder, Churchy. God help me, I think it's Elder." Both men walked along in silence, the horror of the situation bringing back that dreaded time on the island. Kirkgordon remembered seeing the dark wings and red eyes rising from the sea. A thought struck him.

"Indy, these frog-men we saw, how common are they to this place?"

"From the manuscripts I've read, and do remember they are from a much older time, I would say they are not indigenous."

"So they are migrants?"

"At some point. That would be a reasonable assumption," agreed Austerley.

"And if Farthington was working for Dagon and he has his camp around here then you would expect..."

"E-O-D! Dammit, Churchy, they'll be here too. That's why we saw frog-men."

"But they won't be partners anymore. Farthington failed Dagon, killed lots of his followers, took away his established base up in Scotland. This could be useful, Indy. We might not be the only ones looking for Farthington." Kirkgordon chuckled to himself before seeing that Austerley's face had gone white. "What's the matter?"

"Looking for Farthington. He'll be looking for Farthington. Hell, Churchy, who sent him back, who cast him out? Who was the one who went toe-to-toe and sent that thing back to the depths? Me. Bloody me. If he wants Farthington then he'll damn well want me ten times more. And what's more, I have a beacon attached that's gonna send him a signal!"

"That's a point. Is there any way to remove the darkness from it?"

"Not that I know of."

"And Havers' lopping-it-off idea is a non-starter?"

"Of course it's a non-starter. It's my bloody foot."

"But you said you needed rid of it otherwise you'd end up meeting Dagon again." Kirkgordon saw Austerley become more agitated, looking off into the undergrowth of the forest. "Are you saying chopping it off wouldn't work?"

"Work? It's not on the cards, Churchy, understand? I lost it once before and I'm not going through that pain again. I'll sort it out. Maybe up here I'll find someone who can move these things on."

"I hope so. Farthington's enough to have on our plate without Dagon and his frog chorus."

The group continued along the path until tree cover broke without warning and they were facing an enormous gatehouse. On top of it were militia in the same outfits the group on the path had worn. Kirkgordon made a quick count; they numbered at least thirty-five.

There was a large portcullis hovering halfway up the open doorway of the gatehouse and a small team of militia accompanying a man in colourful medieval garb, who appeared to be talking to everyone who was trying to enter the city.

"I'll sort this, Mr Kirkgordon," said Havers, "seeing as I'm quite good with the local lingo."

Kirkgordon nodded but whispered to Austerley, "Go with

him, Indy, I don't trust him."

"I've never trusted him," said Austerley and followed Havers towards the man in the bright clothing.

Kirkgordon felt useless, once again having to wait for the exchange to finish before he could get a translation of what had passed. Austerley informed him that Havers had managed to obtain a thirty-eight hour pass, after which time they would have to vacate the city or spend a night in the cells. The pass was given only because of the extreme need of Nefol. Pleased that they had obtained a much better result than having to attack an entire city's militia, Kirkgordon let Austerley hobble forward to look around the city.

For all his panic about encountering Farthington or Dagon, Kirkgordon noticed that Austerley was once again in his element. This was somewhere ordinary people didn't see and no doubt there were many wondrous and probably terrible sights lurking beneath its surface. But this was no school outing, and Kirkgordon asked Havers and Austerley to look for some accommodation.

Initially the streets were like a shanty town, with many houses made of basic timber or sheet metal, usually taken from something intended for another purpose entirely. Faces peered out from the houses, displaying a variety of eyes, from large bulbous ones that reminded Kirkgordon of the frog-men to others that were mere slits. Occasionally Austerley would veer towards these eyes out of curiosity, but each time Kirkgordon would rein him back in.

Soon the buildings became stout, strong timber constructions with full windows that were draped inside with curtains, and Kirkgordon noticed that the people – no, life forms – that occupied the street were better dressed. On passing a sign with a drawing of a cloaked individual with a rather bloody foot, Austerley insisted to Havers that they would not be going in.

"What's up with you, Indy?" asked Calandra.

"The one-legged vampire! As if."

"What do you mean, Indy?" asked Kirkgordon.

"Havers wants me to go into the one-legged vampire pub. Bloody comedian."

"It's only a pub, Indy. I'm sure there's not..."

"No," insisted Austerley. "Now, can we get on?"

After a short walk, another pub appeared. At least, from the movements of those exiting the establishment, it appeared to be a pub. Havers went inside briefly with Austerley before returning and calling the rest of the group in.

"There are rooms upstairs, Mr Kirkgordon, of which I have acquired three. One for the ladies which adjoins a room that should suit Mr Austerley and yourself. And there is one across the hall which will suit myself, I think."

"Good. Now take Calandra and find us a healer," ordered Kirkgordon.

"No, Mr Kirkgordon."

"No, Havers, you can get the name of the creatures and Nefol's condition from him in this language, and you seem to know enough to cope otherwise. Calandra will make sure you stay on task and not begin to freelance in Farthington's direction."

"Very good, Mr Kirkgordon, I see you are beginning to think like me."

Not so, Havers, thought Kirkgordon, not so. He watched Calandra and Havers leave before taking Nefol upstairs. The rooms were basic but each contained two beds. Kirkgordon laid Nefol down upon one. The girl was breathing and appeared to be in a deep sleep, but earlier attempts to wake her up had failed. There was a pitcher of water in the room, so Kirkgordon poured himself a glass and sat down in a wooden chair near one of the windows. Austerley, seeing the chance to relax, laid down on the second bed and closed his eyes.

Not much to do now but wait, thought Kirkgordon. And for the first time in a while he began to think about Alana and where Farthington could be holding her. First she was in a dungeon and then on a rock face. Then there was a palace and a grave. But everywhere that his dreams took him, Calandra was also there. His eyes drifted from one figure to the next, enjoying the curves despite the peril they represented. He felt himself slipping into a happy stupor as he heard the rhythmic shake of a maraca.

Hang on. A maraca? Kirkgordon's eyes flicked open. Nefol was lying quite still, but Austerley had his shoes and socks off and next to his ordinary white foot, the ebony appendage was vibrating with such a velocity that the bed was shaking and knocking into a nearby dresser. On the dresser, some small rocks in a bowl – a sort of mineral potpourri – were colliding and causing the maraca sound. But all thoughts of rocks and maracas disappeared from Kirkgordon's mind as he realized that although Austerley was fast asleep, his black foot was not.

Kilon

It was the latter part of the day, and outside the night had begun to approach. Kirkgordon listened carefully but he could hear only the rattling of the items on the table. Slowly, he edged out of his seat and took up position at the only door of the room. Standing to one side, he took his bow and placed a single arrow on the string. The coloured flashings indicated a normal arrow. He had insisted to Nefol that he bring some when he restocked the quiver before the journey.

A glance at Austerley's foot showed that it had swollen and was now shaking quite violently. Austerley began to stir, moaning and breathing heavily. Keeping his eye fixed on his partner, Kirkgordon wondered how long Austerley would remain asleep. There were moments when he seemed to be awake, his eyelids opening, but each time he dropped back under. The window's the only way out if anyone takes the door, thought Kirkgordon. It's a two-storey drop. Indy will probably break his legs and how I'll get Nefol away I don't know.

And then he heard a hopping sound. Tiny little splats on the wooden staircase; they had climbed to the rooms. It sounded like someone playing a game of hopscotch while being determined that no one should find out. But there's only one splat, thought Kirkgordon, just the one. If I get the element of surprise I can take him, or it, or whatever. The sound drew closer, and finally a gentle splat stopped right outside the door.

Kirkgordon drew the bow, stepping back slightly so that the door could open. Believing the opener would see Austerley in bed and move to attack him, Kirkgordon reckoned he could nail the creature before it could reach Austerley. He certainly didn't want to fight it in hand-to-hand combat. The frog-men on the island had been very strong and difficult to subdue.

The door swung open easily, gliding to a halt just in time to allow Kirkgordon to maintain his cover. There was a light splatting sound but nothing moved into the room. Kirkgordon held his breath but didn't panic. Austerley's foot was now vibrating wildly and Austerley himself was beginning to come to life. The former professor grunted momentarily before sitting up and opening his eyes wide.

"You!" Austerley screamed. Kirkgordon held his ground but tried to twist his head to see if there was a weapon pointing at Austerley. "I can explain," continued Austerley. "It wasn't my fault. The manuscript was at fault. A poor copy... bad publication... not my fault."

Hell, thought Kirkgordon, it's either Farthington himself or the Dagon roadshow. But that splat sound...

Kirkgordon felt a chill run down his spine and something told him there was danger behind him. He rolled out in front of the doorway then came up on his knees and aimed his bow at the... head, maybe, of the thing that stood there. It stood on a single central leg with a webbed foot at the bottom and was only four feet tall. There were six eyes arranged around the transparent jelly-like head, and arteries and other internal bodily necessities were clearly visible.

"Tell it not to move, Indy, or I'll split its head in two."

"Tell it yourself, it speaks damn good English." An underlying terror could still be heard in Austerley's voice, but Kirkgordon's move had given him some confidence.

"Does it have a name?"

"I do indeed," said the thing, without using any obvious mouth. "'Kilondoneanghnftlykuifop' is how I think you would pronounce it, but the Professor and myself always used 'Kilon' for short, and I think that will suffice."

"How are you speaking?" asked Kirkgordon. "Indy, how's it doing that?"

"Why, the only way I know how. I move the skin in a refined manner thereby causing such fluctuations in the air that the molecules move in a certain way. The said movement is then picked up by your ear. The Professor picked up on it very quickly."

"Indy, how do you know this creature and is it safe?"

"I met it back in our world, Churchy, and I kind of... well I... dropped it and twenty-five of its family into a crevice."

"I didn't know you had it in you to pick a fight and win."

"Well, I was in the process of moving their house by mental teleportation but instead opened up the ground and dropped Kilon and his family together with their house ten miles under the ground. I thought he'd be a bit pissed off, actually."

"Not at all, my dear Professor, you were doing your best. It did take a while to extricate ourselves from the depths of that hole, but you were doing your best," said the creature, remaining in the doorway.

"So what's your purpose in coming here? How did you know Austerley was here?"

"My friend saw you at the outer limits of the city when your friend, the lady with the stick, began to argue with the militia and the moustached man shot them. He was very quick on the trigger and accurate not to kill any of them. Significant but non-lethal hits."

"And how do I know your intentions with Austerley are good? How do I know you aren't here to kill him or deliver him up to someone? Why shouldn't I put you down just to be on the safe side?"

"Because his friend will drop you before you even let that arrow fly." The voice came from behind Kirkgordon and with it a chill ran up his spine. He felt a cold line across his throat but could see nothing from the corner of either eye. "This one smells fresh enough, Kilon."

Kirkgordon let the tension on his bow drop off. "Okay, you have the upper hand, so say your piece."

Kilon hopped into the room, every landing making a quiet splat. The door closed behind him as if by magic and Kirkgordon felt like his mind was catching the last bus to la-la land. At least these are the good guys, he thought.

"There has been some... noise, shall we say, Professor? In the darker streets of the city, there has been talk of the Professor and the Agent coming. And the Archer too, a man looking for his wife but who brings the Angel with him." Kilon kept his eyes fixed on Austerley while he spoke.

"An Angel. I wouldn't tell her that, what do you think, Austerley? She might just put those wings to good use." Kirkgordon tried to chuckle as he spoke but he was too aware of the cold line across his throat.

"Who is talking, Kilon?" asked Austerley.

"They say you are looking for the man-dragon, the one who dines with the Pontiff. The one who brought the guns to our city. Many of the fleshers haven't forgotten that."

"Fleshers?" asked Kirkgordon.

"Yes, those who can be harmed by weapons from your world, the non-spiritual, but not in the godly sense. They don't like these new toys that are bringing servitude to those not of spirit. Something must be done. And I think the Professor will know what to do. A clever man, the Professor, is what I thought. I shall get some help."

"So Farthington has his feet under the table with the authorities. That's not good," stated Kirkgordon. "Alana could be anywhere in this city."

"Farthington?" queried Kilon.

"The man-dragon is known as Farthington to us, or as Zmey Gorynych," Austerley answered. "He kidnapped my friend's wife when we previously had him cornered and has run away from us. So far we have tried to track him and have ended up here, but we weren't sure that he was here."

"Oh, he's here," said Kilon. "And there are many who wish he wasn't."

"Well, I intend to rid this place of him," declared Austerley, in a moment of bravado which caused Kirkgordon to laugh.

"Why do you mock the Professor?" asked Kilon.

"Because he didn't want to come here. So far, he's passed out twice and has only attracted bad things with that damned foot of his."

"Ah, I see you have exchanged feet with someone. You have such a talent, Professor, for the words in the books. But I think you may have chosen the wrong donor this time."

"You don't say," grunted Austerley.

"If I was you, Professor, I'd have someone cut it off quickly and learn to walk without it."

"Nobody is cutting my leg off. Can we get that straight?"

"But it will cause you trouble, Professor. You see, the talk in quiet corners is that they have returned. Returned to cause trouble."

"Who?" asked Kirkgordon.

"The webbed-feet people. Very dark is their world. The creature they worship brings only the black night."

"We saw some frog-men when we arrived in this world," said Kirkgordon.

"Frog-men?" asked Kilon. Austerley made some bizarre noises. "Ah yes, I see the way it's put together now. Yes, Archer, frog-men."

"Then Dagon is looking for me, Churchy. You hear that? Dagon's here."

"Looks like it. But he may not know you're here. It might be Farthington he knows about."

"Archer," said Kilon, "if I know you are here then they will. Nothing hides from the shadow."

Austerley was shaking on the bed. Staring at his foot, he muttered under his breath. Kirkgordon could see Austerley was withdrawing into himself, drawing back from the mammoth danger they now faced, but he needed to salvage something good from this situation.

"Kilon, are you able to heal people?"

"You have need of a healer? If it's the Professor's foot you speak of, then sadly not," answered Kilon.

"No, an associate of mine got bitten by some little furballs with big fangs, called... called... Austerley, what do you call the furballs?" There was a grunt from Austerley followed by more weird noises in another language.

"But of course. Where is the sufferer?"

"On the other bed. I'll take you nearer if this coldness is released from my throat."

"Of course, I think I can see you are the Professor's friend."

Kirkgordon felt the cold disappear from his throat and led Kilon to Nefol's bedside. The monoped creature stared intently at the sleeping girl. Suddenly the room began to hum. It was like a quiet droning in the background and the feeling that the merest of sea breezes was tickling its way past your face. For Kirkgordon it was as if he could drift away, back to more pleasant times, but then the rattling of Austerley's foot broke through all semblance of calm.

"What are you doing, Kilon?" asked Kirkgordon.

"Please don't interrupt my friend when he's working," came a voice from the darkest corners. "At the moment he is assessing how she is and then he will work out how to heal her. He's very good at healing people, isn't he, Professor?"

Austerley nodded as he fought to calm his foot down, to no avail.

Kirkgordon addressed the dark. "But what about Auster… the Professor's foot, why can't he do anything about that?"

"Because, Archer, the girl has been affected by a physical poison, something natural, so to speak, even if you struggle to believe it. The Professor has a spiritual pain. You need a priest."

"A man of God," asked Kirkgordon.

"If that's where your allegiance lies. But there are others who could work on it."

"I'm afraid our priest died saving several of us, including the girl who the foot came from. I could really use him now."

"It is done," interrupted Kilon.

"What's done?" asked Kirkgordon.

"I have stabilized her."

"Stabilized? You didn't even touch her!"

"He doesn't touch people, Churchy. You felt the wind, his presence. He touched her in other ways," informed Austerley.

This was getting to be too much for Kirkgordon. For once, all he wanted was to be stuck in some Middle Eastern market running for his life with his protectee.

"I need to go out and get some items to help her recover fully, Professor, but my friend will remain here to watch over you. Don't worry about the girl, she will be fine in a few hours," said Kilon.

"Where is your friend?" asked Kirkgordon.

"He's in the corner, Archer."

"Which corner?"

"Any corner, any dark space."

"I don't understand."

"Churchy, he's in every corner. He belongs in the dark places, the spots the children fear to look into. Sometimes you are just plain ignorant. It's a wonder you managed to get here."

"Get here. A wonder how I got here." Kirkgordon rounded on Austerley. "You lie there with a damned foot that acts as a beacon to the weird and wonderful, no offence guys, and brings us frog-men, furballs and now the good doctor and his... his... what the hell is it?"

"Bwgan," said Kilon.

"Bwhat?"

"Bogeyman, Churchy," spat Austerley. "He's just a bogeyman."

"Hey-ho, that's just dandy then. You just remember who's keeping Havers from lopping that foot off before you get on your high horse again."

"Shall I retire and retrieve the required items for the girl's healing, Archer?" asked Kilon.

"Yes... yes, please do. And thank you. Sorry if I seem on edge. It's just that I'm finding things a bit weird and my wife's life is on the line."

"They do say there is a woman with the dragon. I shall see what I can find out, since you are a friend of the Professor," said Kilon before leaving the room. Austerley grinned at Kirkgordon, reminding him that it was the Professor who had the connections.

"Time to just sit and wait then," said Kirkgordon. "I take it the bogeyman is still here?"

"I'm here."

"I wish he wasn't," groaned Austerley. "This foot of mine just won't settle."

A Familiar Church

Havers emerged from another shop, shaking his head at Calandra. This was the fifth supposed apothecary they had investigated, but no one seemed to know what to do about a bite from the furballs. There was anger brewing within Calandra at the uselessness of this city and she was beginning to regret coming here. Surely the human doctors from Churchy's realm could sort this out. They would at least have more interest.

"Where now then, Havers?"

"Well, my dear, I am beginning to think this is a wild goose chase and we may need to think beyond the basic healers of the town. Possibly we may garner better information from the holy men. There was a temple to what looked like a reasonable god a few streets back," said Havers.

"Okay, but let's be quick. Nefol's condition may be getting worse for all we know."

"I am moving with some alacrity for a man of my age, I'll have you know. But yes, by all means, a little push to our efforts may help things along."

The streets of the town were busy and in this particular area were based on cobblestones which were well maintained. Various carts and horses were being driven along the main thoroughfares and Calandra had to be careful where she trod, given the amount of manure scattered along the road. Soon they arrived at the temple, which was really a glorified set of lodgings. As had been their plan, Havers went to call on the residents while Calandra kept watch from across the street.

Havers knocked on the door of the lodgings. It opened and to Calandra's surprise a human peered out. There were plenty of humanoid persons in the town but Havers had been the only actual human she'd seen since they had left their rooms.

"He has a price for her return. No, don't look round or the blade will remove your head." The voice came from behind.

"He has a price? Since when did he need money?" asked Calandra.

"There is no need for money, Miss, but can you not feel it in the wind? The one who would be his master is not pleased. He roams forever in the dark, waiting to be released, waiting to wreak havoc on the world, on many worlds." The voice was low and husky and Calandra thought she had heard it before on a late night radio show that she had listened to while babysitting Austerley.

"So he knows we are here. He must need us bad or I would be dead."

"Not you. He needs Austerley. It has been sent and it is coming. In the week ahead the days will darken and the fear will accompany it, but that will be nothing to when it is unleashed. If Kirkgordon wants to see his wife again, he will get Austerley to destroy it." The voice sounded urgent, as if it wasn't sure that the contract would be signed.

"And how do we know what it is that we are to destroy?"

"Austerley will know it when he sees it. The rip in time, the fracture that it seeks to come through. In the Rock Temple. Tell Austerley that the one steeped in darkness comes."

Calandra shook her head. "You think I am just going to go running back to the gang with some cock and bull story about Farthington being in trouble and for our help he'll be happy to release Alana? I am eight hundred years old and have seen a con or two in my time."

The voice became intense and angry. "Tell Austerley. Tell him of Captain Orne's downfall. And it will not stop here, for it searches the realms. Tell him. For all our sakes, tell him!"

Then came a silence which made Calandra think about looking round. But before she could investigate whether the voice had left the vicinity, Havers emerged from the building across the road.

Calandra turned her attentions to her feet to keep Havers from seeing her face. Part of her was worried that any notion of dealing with Farthington, and in particular saving him, would cut against Havers' plans.

"Any luck, Havers?"

"Actually, we may be in luck. The head priest of this order seems to know a method but he has had to consult some of his other priests. I said I would pop out and bring you in to hear about it. Friendly chap, been serving this city for a number of years. His order is originally from Hurkangdra. Ah, I see that rings a bell with you."

"Yes, it does. I was there for nearly ten years when I was about three hundred, I think. A quiet realm with some underlying problems."

"Yes, the priest said so. He said that they were based there originally but they felt called to come here. Or rather, a message from their deity advised them to come here."

"And what deity is that?"

"I'm not exactly sure. The name is quite awkward, but they

certainly seemed harmless."

"After you, then."

The pair walked across the road and Havers knocked on the door. After being led inside, they were taken to an old room which was dank and dusty. In a circle sat six hooded figures of whom only one removed its cowl when the pair entered the room. Havers began to talk in the language of the city and Calandra looked around. There were several pictures on the wall which showed Hurkangdra. She recognized the sea rocks being shaped on the anvil and the Flattenburg fish being eaten on the shores. A speciality of that region.

There was a small altar at the top end of the room, probably just large enough to hold a person lying down. Would be cold though, thought Calandra. She could hear Havers conversing as she walked closer to the altar and spied some writing on the side. It was in older Hurkanda, which was handy as that was what she had spoken for those ten years. The modern language was bewildering to her.

There were three words in large letters of the Hurkanda script and they certainly weren't normal ones. The second word was the easiest and meant group or meeting. The third one was bizarre, not a word she could grab at all. The first word she knew in her depths. It wasn't a common one but she knew, she was sure. Come on Cally, old girl, you can do it. She stared at the letters in stone. Arcane. Maybe arcane. Or cryptic or magical. Mystic, that was it, mystic. The mystic group something or other.

The third word was eluding her and she turned to watch Havers listening to the priest. He briefly looked up and smiled, indicating that all was okay. Turning back to the letters, she realized that the last word was two words rammed together.

Fish was the first part and the second... This was like that blasted game Kirkgordon went on about playing with his children.

Ah yes, deity. That was it. Fish-deity or Fish God. The mystic group of the fish god. Bit weird that but then Hurkangdra was a place where fishing had ruled. And drinking of course. Mustn't forget the drinking.

Havers touched her shoulder and made Calandra jump round.

"Well, that's settled, Miss Calandra. They are just going to get a few things and then we will be off. I said we could take them to Nefol but they suggested they go and get her. I'm going to go with them, of course. They said you should stay and they could look at your wounds from the journey."

"I dare say it will be to Austerley's taste here," said Calandra.

"How so?" asked Havers.

"Hurkangdra is mainly coastal and they have all sorts of tall tales. Do you see the pictures? Takes me back. Even this old altar here. I can read the script, Havers. Look, from right to left, like the Chinese. Mystic group of the Fish-god."

"Mystic group? Could be mystic like arcane? And an organized group? An order."

"Probably."

"We need to go, dear lady. Ready your weapon."

"Why, Havers? It's just Hurkangdra culture."

"Esoteric Order of Dagon. He is a fish god in many cultures. I believe that says Esoteric Order of Dagon."

"The island church. No," whispered Calandra.

Havers strode up behind one of the hooded priests and pulled down its deep hood. An elliptical green, slimy head was revealed. The head spun round and bulbous eyes looked at Havers.

"EOD, my dear, it's definitely EOD." And he drove a concealed knife into the frog-man. As he let the frog-man fall to the ground, Havers pulled his pistols from inside his garb. Before he could fire, one of the priests swung an arm and caught Havers in the mouth, sending him crashing backwards. The roof of the room was too low for a frog-man to leap and the restriction forced them into small, controlled hops. This saving grace allowed Calandra to step in front of Havers with her staff. As she clobbered a frog-man with the end of the staff, she heard Havers shout a warning and she spun the staff behind her without looking. A dull thwack onto coarse skin told her she had hit the target and the subsequent thud confirmed it had been a good strike.

"We need to go, Havers."

"An excellent suggestion, my dear, one I have already made, but we are somewhat cornered at the moment. Any suggestions?"

"Apart from fight our way out, not a lot." Another frog-man felt a blow under his chin, but Calandra knew she would tire eventually and she had no idea how many of these creatures there were.

"There are reasons I run the department, my dear. Now close your eyes on my mark." Havers threw a small device from behind her and she saw it land amongst the frog-men. "Mark!"

Shutting her eyes, Calandra kept her staff swinging in front of her for protection. Despite pulling her eyelids tight, her vision still registered a bright white. And milliseconds later came the bang. She heard a voice beside her, but it was unintelligible because of the ringing in her ears. Something grabbed her arm and she barely held on to her staff with her other hand. Her feet tripped forward but she had the dexterity to remain upright while the unknown force dragged her on.

She opened her eyes and saw Havers' hand pulling her. Around wooden corridors they ran, in what seemed like a maze. Havers would have memorized the way in, thought Calandra, so that must be blocked. A frog-man appeared in front of them but she saw a knife shoot straight into the amphibian's throat and he collapsed to the ground.

Slowly, her ears were recovering and she was grateful to hear the drumming of their feet on the wooden floorboards. Having no idea where she was, she trusted Havers' arm as they began to climb stairs.

"Watch your feet, Miss Calandra, these are damned wide."

"Meant for hoppers then, Havers."

"Ah, you are hearing again, good. My apologies, but I didn't have time to warn you of everything."

"Can we not slow down a moment? I don't hear them behind us." The floor and walls of the building were now stone and there was a mustiness in the air born more of disuse than decay.

"I am afraid not. In my attempts to render aid to Nefol I told the priest our location. Once they fail to find us they will no doubt make their way directly to Mr Kirkgordon. I have a feeling they knew Mr Austerley was nearby anyway, from some of the comments they made to each other. Unfortunately I realized this after I had disclosed the location."

"Dammit Havers, they'll just kill Nefol and Churchy. Austerley's their baby."

"I am aware, my dear. Round to the right there."

She turned as directed and they found a wooden door in front of them. Calandra leaned up against it, listening for sounds beyond.

"There's a low chant. But it sounds distant. Maybe only one or two," said Calandra.

"Listen behind," advised Havers. There was the sound of a multitude of splats, many hopping feet landing on stone. "We can't go back. I think forward will be easier."

"After three then, element of surprise. You take the right, me the left." Havers nodded. "One, two, three!"

Calandra drove the door open with her foot and led Havers into the room. It was a small, dimly lit hall with many stained glass windows. They had entered from a door midway along one side of the hall. From their left came the smell of burning incense and on a small stage was a hooded figure who was chanting. While this was not a large issue, the fact that the other hundred hooded figures who had been crouched in prayer were now rapidly rising to face them undoubtedly was.

Looking behind her, Calandra saw frog-men entering the corridor that she and Havers had come from. Calandra scanned the room, seeking a way out, as the figures in the room began to move towards them. There were numerous banners adorning the room, mainly decrepit structures devoid of their former colours, but all hanging from a narrow parapet that ran round the room.

"Havers, out of the stained glass window. We can climb up the banners and round the parapet. Follow me!"

Calandra turned and grabbed the nearest banner, rapidly climbing up its length. As her hand reached the parapet, she looked down to see Havers climbing behind her. He had reached a height of some ten feet above the ground and she reckoned him safe from the horde below.

She hauled herself onto the parapet then dropped a hand down for Havers, but a frog-man sprang up from the crowd and clutched at him. Calandra swung her hand down further and Havers reached out desperately with his left hand, his right still grasping the banner. Their fingers touched briefly but the banner ripped and Havers fell with the frog-man into the crowd below.

"Havers!" A cold feeling tore up her spine but Calandra knew she had to move. In her older days of conflict she had lost many a colleague and it never felt acceptable. But this old shieldmaiden knew how to compartmentalize the pain and take action.

Standing up on the narrow parapet, she began to race along it towards the nearest stained glass window. A frog-man leapt from the crowd up to her height but got the hard end of her staff as a reward. It rocked her balance briefly but she recovered and ran on. The window was slightly offset into the wall and she was glad of this as she reached the alcove.

A black figure with wings and red eyes looked back from the window and for a second she was taken back to the island and the demon who had risen from the sea.

"Bastard! You evil bastard." She looked round into the crowd hoping to see Havers fighting his way out but there was just a mass of hooded figures. "Sorry, boss!" Calandra turned to face the window, ready to smash it out and look for a ledge on the far side. But without warning she was hit from the rear and tumbled forward. The glass smashed and Calandra, in the clutches of a frog-man, began to fall.

Someone's Baby

Calandra tumbled forward onto a small ledge with the frog-man holding her tight. They rolled over, teetering on the brink of a large drop. Her ribs felt like they were about to snap as the powerful arms of the creature squeezed her tight, but her staff, trapped as it was by those arms, provided some relief. Leaning forward, she bit into the frog-man's arm, tearing out a large lump of green flesh. There was a hideous croak and the arm loosened its grip. Exploiting this weakness, Calandra prised the two arms apart and rolled over one last time with the creature. She clutched the ledge with her right hand, staff held in her left, and shrugged hard, letting the frog-man fall over the edge. Her momentary sense of relief was dashed as she felt a webbed hand grab her foot.

She kicked down hard with her other foot, but her arm was in agony. The frog-man was resisting and even managed to place another webbed hand onto the same leg. This is enough, thought Calandra, and she smacked her staff down hard on the creature's head. The webbed hands released and she saw the creature fall. The drop was more than considerable and it was some five seconds before the sickening splat could be heard.

A further splurge followed as two bulbous eyes appeared in front of her. Another frog-man had been following her progress. To pull herself up was difficult enough, but she would also be totally exposed to her attacker and would surely be thrown from the ledge. Calandra twisted so her left side hung away from the face of the wall and she began to spin her staff in her free hand. Hundreds of years of practice had helped the staff become a part of her and soon the ends of the staff gleamed white hot.

"So long, Kermit," she yelled and drove the edge of the staff into the wall. The brickwork melted around the end of the staff, which slowly descended the wall with Calandra hanging from it. She ignored the pain in her arms and looked below for an escape. There were hooded figures emerging from the bottom of the tower, some running and others hopping.

Glancing around, she saw that a smaller tower joined onto the one she was descending. Leaning into her staff, Calandra steered closer to this second tower before stopping her descent by jamming her feet against the wall. Pulling the staff from the wall, she back-flipped and landed on the parapet surrounding the top of the second tower. She ran round the parapet without looking back down. On the other side was a large paved area with a wooden door on the far side. There was no one about so Calandra ran up to the door. After listening for a moment, she opened it and stepped inside.

Calandra was in a small closet with perforated walls. The air was moist and humid and steam hung around her, even in this confined space. She peered through the holes and saw a desperate situation. A young woman dressed in a white robe was being led to a platform overhanging a large pool. This was the source of the steam. Above the pool hung a rope, and over twenty hooded figures chanted as the woman was taken towards the fixture.

I can't take on twenty of them, thought Calandra, but that

poor girl's a goner if I don't do something. She watched as the figures tied the girl's wrists up and pulled the far end of the rope, lifting the girl until she hung over the centre of the pool. Large pieces of meat were thrown into the pool which began to bubble and froth. Oh, this is not good.

The hooded figures withdrew quickly from the room through a door on the farthest side from Calandra.

I can't leave her. Churchy didn't leave me, instead he came back. Nefol wouldn't think much of me either if I just ran. Oh hell, I'd better just get on with it.

Calandra pushed open a panel in the perforated hide and cautiously stepped towards the pool's edge. The woman was shaking, sick with terror.

"Let's get you down," said Calandra. There was no response. Okay, let's try another language. She tried another five languages before giving up. The water continued to bubble and Calandra studied the walls for any point from which she could grab the rope. She had hoped to get the girl back by pulling on the line the hooded figures had used, but they had let the end swing out over the pool. In fact that was puzzling Calandra. There must be some sort of magic involved, because the woman should have dropped into the pool by now.

Around the walls were pictures of creatures. Looking more closely, Calandra saw that there was in fact only one creature depicted, but she had been confused by the many heads in each image. Now she saw that they emerged from one body. A hydra. EOD. Mother Hydra. She would always remember Austerley's cries in the pub on the island. Dagon's worshippers were here in force.

The woman was shrieking now and yelled in a language Calandra didn't understand. It felt like the room temperature was increasing, and the water became violent and splashed over the edge of the pool. There was a smell in the air: dampness, mouldy walls, a fustiness. From her position, two thirds of the pool were out of sight to her. But she felt something behind her. The hairs on her arm tingled and from the corner of her eye she saw something move. Turning, she saw first one head and then a second. Then she was taking in the full aspect of a red-skinned hydra.

Anyone looking at Calandra might have deduced she was sweating in the heat. However, her pallor remained pale, almost white. Her skin was so cold that condensation was forming on her face, at the roots of her hair and across the bare skin revealed by her top. The water dripped into her eyes, but they remained wide open as the full horror of what she was about to face struck her.

One head struck out from the side and took the end of her staff on its jaw. All at once the other heads began to strike at her and Calandra moved with a speed born from hundreds of years of practice and experience. She struck at least four of the heads in the first three seconds before receiving a bite to her thigh. Trying to muffle a yell, she ran to the corner of the room. Resetting her stance, she began to spin the staff, generating white heat from its ends. A head snapped at her and was taken clean off. Green blood spattered her face but she was emotionless as she drove forward with the staff.

The loose neck that now ended in a stump withdrew to the rear of the creature, where the head regrew with amazing speed. I'm just buying time doing this, thought Calandra. This thing could keep regrowing all day.

The hydra was only twice Calandra's height and a notion struck Calandra. This was a baby, a toddler at best. Let's hope

Mum's not around. But, baby or not, I doubt I could keep it entertained until the hooded folk come back to make sure it has done its job. I'm going to need to do something quick and effective.

Calandra stopped spinning the staff and held it over her knee. With a swift push down, she snapped it, taking the two pieces, one in either hand. And then she paused in a defensive stance, staring at the creature. The hydra held its ground, assessing what action she was going to take. Then three of its heads turned back towards the woman hanging over the pool, and Calandra struck.

Breaking into an immediate sprint, she ran directly at the body of the hydra. The four heads that remained watching her struck out but she batted them away with the pieces of her staff, scalding the faces. The other three heads swung round to attack but were too late as Calandra leapt and buried the ends of both pieces of her staff into the belly of the beast.

The creature howled with several of its mouths but one managed to grab Calandra by the ankle. It thrashed wildly about with Calandra attached. She sustained some severe bangs to her sides and lost her bearings completely. Her vision was becoming blurred. Calandra fought to raise her arms over her head and then felt herself collide with something other than part of the building.

The girl who had been hanging over the water yelled as Calandra struck her. The rope buckled and then fell limp, causing the girl to fall. With her hands still bound, she made a desperate bid to grasp hold of something but caught only the teeth of the mouth that was holding Calandra by the foot. The strain on its jaw caused the hydra to let go its prey, and Calandra and the girl dropped into the water.

Calandra tried to look through the water but it was too turbulent. Blood was also beginning to cloud the water and Calandra knew some of it must be her own. Normally her blood clotted quickly when it was exposed to the air, but in the heat of the pool her ankle just kept on bleeding. I must get back to the surface, she thought, glad that she had taken a gulp of air just before she hit the water.

The sound of something large entering the pool reached her before she felt the water above pushing her further down. Although she couldn't see what had caused the disturbance, the sheer volume involved indicated that it had to be the hydra itself. She had buried the sticks in deep, and a dark green colour began to spread through the water.

Calandra kicked hard with her feet and her head caught some of the hydra's skin. Feeling around it, she found it to be rough enough to pull herself along. Something nudged her side and she reckoned it was a head, but the blow was extremely weak. Then her hand felt a piece of wood and she grabbed one of her sticks, yanking it out from the creature. There followed a modest thrashing from the beast, but Calandra hung onto her position and tried to find the other piece of her staff.

A desperate hand grasped onto her leg and Calandra reached down to find it was humanoid. This meant letting go of her piece of staff but she knew the girl wouldn't have much oxygen left. Holding the girl with one hand, she climbed up the hydra, which had become very still in the water. Her climbing hand landed on her other staff piece and she pulled it out but had to let it go. As she climbed, the hydra was descending. Calandra kicked away from the creature and swam to the surface. Breaking through, she gasped for air and then pulled the girl to the surface after her. Sucking in the humid air, she swam to the side of the pool and threw the girl unceremoniously onto the poolside. With two hands on the poolside, Calandra pulled herself out and took a moment to catch her breath.

The girl was lying exposed with her robe open and ripped at waist height. Well, she can't run around like that, thought Calandra, and took off her jacket. Calandra stood the girl up, stripped off the torn upper part of her robe and placed the jacket on her shoulders.

"This is a time to be glad you don't have my bust," said Calandra, zipping the jacket up. The girl looked at her, bemused. So, she's in shock, not really surprising. Grabbing the remnants of the robe, Calandra tied it around the girl's hips, allowing her modesty to be preserved.

Those hoodies are going to be back soon, thought Calandra, and we need to be out of here. There's no way back from where I came and this tower must be being searched. I'm still standing though, unlike Havers, poor sod. Let's hope this girl is a help.

Calandra looked around the room for any sort of weapon, but apart from the pictures on the wall and the platform, there was nothing. Then she noticed two pieces of wood in the green coloured bubbling water, floating towards the poolside. Sweet, she thought, I reckoned you were gone. She took the pieces and jammed them together. To the girl's surprise, they became a single piece of wood.

"Neat trick, huh?" said Calandra. The girl just looked bemused and frightened. And then there was a knock at the door.

Dagon's Coming

Kirkgordon sat on the chair close to the window, keeping one eye out the window and the other on the sleeping Nefol. Austerley was still wriggling in annoyance with his foot, its vibration due to the presence of the bogeyman, despite Kirkgordon encouraging the creature to position itself as far away as possible from Austerley. Time was turning slowly as they awaited the return of Kilon. Outside, night had truly fallen and Kirkgordon was beginning to wonder if Calandra and Havers were alright. But he knew his ice maiden would search all night to help the girl lying in the bed across from him.

And we still have to get Alana, he thought. The last time he had left her, things were going better, but that was before Dillingham. The night when he had come downstairs after tucking the children into bed to find her in the skimpiest of dressing gowns seemed far off, as did the kids finding their parents lying together asleep on the floor the following morning.

The physical had spoken for both of them when the words had been so hard to come by. After all, how can you explain creatures in the depths of a grave, men turning into dragons and demons rising from the sea? But he knew what really bothered her. She had always been able to know him better than he knew himself and she had called it. Deep down, he was enjoying the action, the adventure. And this employment from Havers was giving him that kick he had missed so much when he wound up being just a bodyguard. Maybe some professions shouldn't have families.

"Hey, shadow man," called Kirkgordon to the bogeyman, "how many people round here wear habits?"

"Habits?" came a voice from somewhere behind him.

"Yes, like monks, you know, holy men."

"Well," continued the low voice, "there are several temples whose acolytes would be in white or maybe even red."

"These are black. And… and… Oh hell! Austerley up! We need to get out of here."

"What's got into you?" asked Austerley. "We just need to wait for Kilon and he'll heal Nefol and then we can find someone to—"

Kirkgordon grabbed Austerley by his collar and forced him to stand. "One of those bastards is hopping. And Kermit's bringing the Muppet show right here!"

Austerley's face turned white and he began to shake. "EOD, it's EOD, Churchy. Dagon's coming, coming for me. We need to go. Mother Hydra, Dagon! Like before, Churchy, in the crypt. You didn't look in his eyes, you never looked!"

"Shut up and let me think. It's too late to go out the front door. Shadow man, watch our tails. I'll need to carry Nefol." Kirkgordon slung the girl over his shoulder. Well, it was nothing to carrying Austerley. "We go through the door and turn right down the corridor. We'll get to the back of the building, jump out of a window and then vanish into the streets."

Opening the bedroom door, Kirkgordon turned right and

headed down the corridor. He felt Austerley's presence behind him right until he began to make his way down the corridor. Whipping his head round, he saw Austerley proceeding in the opposite direction.

"What the hell are you doing? They're coming that way!"

"It's not me, Churchy. It's the foot! The foot's taking me."

Kirkgordon saw a large shadow loom across the wall and it seemed to grab Austerley's good leg. There then followed the rather bizarre sight of Austerley on his backside, moving down the corridor towards Kirkgordon and Nefol. The black foot was pointing in the opposite direction, straining against the shadow which was pulling Austerley down the corridor. The result was the professor performing mobile splits while his head rocked back and forward, bouncing off the corridor wall. Damn, that's gotta hurt!

Kirkgordon resisted the urge to watch the comical side show and continued down the hall, which ended in a cul-de-sac of three doors. He tried the door on his left. Locked. He tried the middle door. Locked as well. The door on the right opened to reveal an empty closet. Checking behind him, he saw Austerley still being dragged legs akimbo down the hall, looking almost white and babbling about Mother Hydra being in pursuit. The black foot was shaking and throbbing as it pulled in the opposite direction.

Nothing for it, thought Kirkgordon, and he gave the middle door an almighty kick. The door was insubstantial and Kirkgordon's foot sailed right through it, trapping him. Turning his back to it, he battered the door with his elbows and it splintered quite easily. As the last piece gave way, he stumbled over the wreckage and toppled into the room, dropping Nefol from his shoulder. She rolled across the floor.

When it came to questions of how other species copulated, Kirkgordon had drawn down the curtains of his mind and retired for the night. But in the room was a bed and on the bed was a couple. What particular species of couple, he didn't know. How the male, if that was indeed the male, was causing the female to howl like that he didn't know. He knew roughly what they were doing but it wasn't like anything he had done. Or seen done. Or even heard about.

The blue-skinned male stood up. Kirkgordon had assumed this was the male but then, despite the creature's nakedness, there was no evidence as such to confirm this theory. The female had thrown a cover over herself and was shouting in a language Kirkgordon didn't understand. English and French weren't high on the schooling checklist this side of the portal.

Kirkgordon glanced back through the door to see Austerley being dragged towards him by the shadow, followed by an array of hoods at the far end of the corridor. Kirkgordon drew his bow and fired an arrow down the corridor. He heard the roar of a giant with a club and the sound of some frog-heads being pummelled. But then he felt a blow to the side of his own head.

Kirkgordon rolled with the strike, enabling him to clear his attacker. As he looked up he saw the blue creature just as the shadow descended upon it. Its lover howled and the creature began to crumble in terror before being dispatched to the far wall with the brush of a shadowy hand.

"Out of the window, Archer!"

Kirkgordon stood groggily and pulled Nefol onto his shoulder again. The window frame was wooden with a glass pane and Kirkgordon used the point of his bow to smash through it. Looking down, he saw a cart of what appeared to be straw. He swung his legs out the window, then glanced back before letting himself and Nefol drop the single storey. His last view was of some hooded figures reaching the door and Austerley yelling as he was dragged across the room.

As soon as Kirkgordon's legs hit the cart, his nostrils were assaulted by a gross smell. It reminded him of running through the sewers but the stench was stronger. Ah, shit! Literally. With an unwieldy splat, Austerley's backside sent more of the cart's contents into the air. A shadow descended the wall.

"Grab Austerley, Bogey! We need to lose the frogs. They'll just hop down from up there."

Kirkgordon slung Nefol over his shoulder again and almost ran into a frog-man as it landed in front of him. Without stopping, he grabbed an arrow from his quiver and drove it into the creature's leg. On his way past he saw the frog-man's face turn the grey of marble.

The bogeyman, following behind and dragging Austerley, slipped round the newly formed statue of the frog-man. However, he wasn't accustomed to manoeuvring loads and Austerley's head cracked off the marble, knocking him senseless. Kirkgordon headed for the nearest alley without turning round. Once inside it, he ran from one alley to another, criss-crossing and double-tracking back to confuse his pursuers. After a breathless ten minutes, he stopped in a quiet alley, panting hard, and set Nefol down gently against the wall.

"I think we lost them," he said to the air. "I take it that as Austerley is now here, albeit knocked out, you managed to keep up with me."

"Your friend is quite a burden, but I managed, Archer."

"Good. We'll take five right here. I think we lost them anyway as his foot has gone down. It's barely throbbing now." Kirkgordon thought for a moment. "This is a damned mess,

Bogey. Do you know where we are?"

"Roughly, Archer, roughly."

"Good, so you'll be able to get us to your friend?"

"Oh, yes," came the deep voice.

"I'm totally out of my depth here, trying to sneak around. It's Dagon's city, so it's no wonder they found us so easily."

"I think you overestimate Dagon's influence. He has no control here and the numbers of frog-men we have encountered is not normal. I think they found us by another method, one which if we do not solve will bring them here again."

"Austerley's foot. So, what? We just get rid of it?"

"You saw it, Archer. It moved towards them. It has an evil that sought its own kind. They will come again because the foot is drawing them here."

"But there's no way I am going to chop his foot off."

"Well then, we shall be hunted by these creatures and there is no doubt a horde of them concealed here in the city. I do not give our chances of survival high odds. Well, your chances, actually, I can slope into any dark corner. You really need—."

"Shush!" ordered Kirkgordon. The bogeyman fell silent and the sound of splatting feet could be heard. "Dammit," he said under his breath.

"They come. I told you. And now you will be caught." There seemed to be a weight in the air as if something was thinking heavily. "I cannot let Kilon's friend be captured."

Without further warning, a shadow circled Austerley's leg and Kirkgordon saw the foot snap off at the ankle. The was a sickening crack as the bone split. Kirkgordon stood in shock as a shadowy hand threw the blackened foot away.

Austerley woke up screaming. "Argh! My foot, my bloody foot, arrgghhhhhh!"

Kirkgordon raced to the newly created stump to see if he could help but the rejected foot caught his attention. It was coming back towards them. In what he would remember only as the most surreal event in his life, Kirkgordon was kicked in the forehead by the singular foot. The foot then moved towards Austerley and stifled his cries by placing itself on his throat. Austerley's hands shot to the foot but he began to choke.

"Help, I'm getting killed by my own foot." Austerley's legs were thrashing wildly and Kirkgordon staggered over to help him. Pulling hard, Kirkgordon could not understand the incredible leverage the foot had. He couldn't move it. Then a pair of shadowy hands surrounded his and with the next pull the foot became loose. Extending their pull, the bogeyman and Kirkgordon managed to throw the foot down the alley.

"Get round the corner," shouted Kirkgordon. "Take them both and then hang onto a wall or something. It's going to get draughty."

Several hoods were appearing at the far end of the alley as Kirkgordon drew his bow with one of his vortex arrows. As soon as he saw that Nefol and Austerley's bodies had been dragged around the corner behind him, he fired the arrow into the ground at the end of the alley. The wind rose up and a large vortex formed. Several hooded figures disappeared into the swirling blackness, but the foot held firm.

As the wind increased, Kirkgordon saw the foot begin to slide towards the vortex but it was leaving behind a black liquid in the air. The foot, bloodied and bruised, sailed into the darkness and Kirkgordon watched horrified as the blackness started to move towards him. Soon the liquid reached him and began to engulf his face.

He saw a pair of red eyes set deep into a black face. Two

enormous wings with sharp talons reached out from the torso. The demon sat on top of a ruined tower surrounded by countless bodies, mutilated and broken. Blood flowed like a river across the dead, and a high-pitched wailing destroyed all other sounds. He saw Havers skewered with a stake, Austerley hanging by his neck, Nefol with her back broken into right angles and Calandra disembowelled. All was despair. All was death. The air stank of corpses and his own flesh began to shred and fall away. A heaviness overcame him and he sank to his knees.

Stand!

"No, it can't be. It will not come to this." Tears flowed down Kirkgordon's face and he fought to keep himself from rolling into a miserable ball on the floor. He drew his hands into fists and planted them in front of him. Pushing down hard, he forced himself to stand and look up at the demon sat on high. The eyes were from the island. He remembered them rising to the surface, full of hatred and dark loathing. His body was shaking, just as Austerley's had upon that platform, and a deep dark mood had overtaken his mind. Was there no beacon, no light amongst this display of evil? Dear God, help me. Wherever you are, just help me now.

"Stand!"

The voice had come from behind. It was firm but calm, like a resolute rallying call on a goal-line defence. Something gripped his shoulder. He tilted his head to look but the object gripping him was so incredibly bright he had to stop. Kirkgordon smiled.

Getting to his feet, Kirkgordon looked ahead past all the devastation to the demon. There was no glimmer of a cheeky smile from the beast, no cocky voice, just plain despair. Bland and remorseless. There was nothing to like about this devil. Inside, Kirkgordon shook and fought to keep the oppression from his mind. Again the voice spoke and again he felt the hand on his shoulder.

"Stand!"

As Kirkgordon stood looking at Dagon, he felt the hand leave his shoulder. At first his legs began to buckle, until the light that had been on his shoulder moved in front of him. Placing a hand up to avoid the glare, he watched the edges of its progress. The brightness moved past Calandra and he saw her stand, magnificent again, face determined. One minute Nefol was broken and then she was standing alert, her face showing that sullen disappointment of a teenager as she looked at Kirkgordon, which made him laugh. Pale, hanging Austerley became the shambling professor he had seen when they first met. And Havers stood too. But he was still skewered. Still bleeding.

The darkness began to rise and Kirkgordon felt the oppression lift from his mind. He took his bow in hand and took an arrow from his quiver. The flashings were white and glinted in the bleak landscape. He drew and shot at the demon on high. The arrow pierced the creature's left wing and a pit of fire opened beneath. For a moment it seemed Dagon would rise on his wings but instead he toppled into the fiery pit, the smell of which came on a sulphuric wind to Kirkgordon's nostrils.

And then he was back in the street with the vortex. He could hear the wind, the cries of frog-men disappearing into the opening. But he couldn't see. Reaching to his face with his hands, he touched the blackness that had enveloped him. Pulling hard, he found it wouldn't move but instead just entangled his hands. Scraping hard around his left eye he found a small gap and opened his eye. The vortex was at its peak but he could tell it would soon diminish.

This had better work, Kirkgordon thought, and he ran

straight at the vortex. He got right to the edge of the vortex and bent forward into the swirling stramash. The darkness began to slip from his face and he held his position, feeling none of the vortex's effects as he was the one who had drawn the arrow. As the blackness peeled from his face, he was able to look around and saw that he had no feet, his body stopping at the torso. So, part of him was here and part back in the real world. Well, in that world, anyway.

There was complete blackness around except for several frog-men swirling uncontrollably. Although their bulbous eyes were those of an amphibian, Kirkgordon swore he could see terror in them. A terror born of having seen an approaching doom. Then, coming towards him in the blackness, was a bear. It opened its mouth and roared. A passing frog-man was grabbed by a crab's claw that was emerging from the side of the bear. The creature grew in size as it came closer, and Kirkgordon remembered the street fight in Dillingham. As a second claw came at him from the side he withdrew the top half of his body from the vortex.

The wind was dying and the opening was beginning to shrink as Kirkgordon wondered just where the other side of the vortex was. In these last few years he had had to ask this sort of question too many times and it wasn't helping his mind one bit. As long as they stay there, he thought.

Cries from faraway streets caused him to break free from his thoughts and he realized he needed to get away before anyone nearby felt brave enough to take a look. Turning around, Kirkgordon exited the street at the far end and found a large shadow overlooking his two friends.

"Right, Bogeyman, get us to Kilon and fast. We really don't need to be on the street and Austerley needs some attention."

*

Calandra opened the door of the pool room and was relieved to find an empty annex. On the far side were some cupboards and on opening them she found some white robes. As if she would dress in that! A further search produced some grey habits like the frog-men wore and Calandra took two of them, throwing one to the girl she had rescued. The girl nodded and put on the robe. Calandra's staff was too long to hide so she broke it in two and carried the pieces within her habit. Now to make a move before anyone came back. There were two doors from the annexe other than that which she had used to enter. One had a black door with many bolts; the other was a flimsy affair. The black door won.

There were large stone steps, too large for a human to descend comfortably, leading into the dark, dank gloom below. The walls were damp and the musty odour almost made Calandra choke. The whole ambiance reminded Calandra of something. She looked closely at the walls and saw that the structure wasn't very old but still had an underlying wetness. It was like the building had been dropped into a marshland, and yet they were high up a tower. The smells and tastes of the island came back to her.

The steps were distinctly wet in the middle, as if hikers had walked over them after tramping through the bogs. But on closer examination, the footprint turned out to be a flipper-print. The island... Innsmouth... Dagon... EOD... oh, no! Calandra's head swam at the thought. She had expected Farthington and a proper scrap but she had hoped, prayed, never to see that demon again. Poor Austerley. The demon would be looking for him.

The terror started to grab her mind and Calandra was forced to do and not think. Signalling the girl behind her to keep following, she descended the steps which, after a few spirals, opened out into a corridor. Calandra walked deftly along the cold floor until she reached two more wooden doors. There were voices coming from behind one. Or rather, there were croaks. The other room seemed to be in silence and Calandra cautiously opened the door. Inside was what looked like a store cupboard with some shelving, most of it collapsing. A large headstone lay against the back wall and Calandra signalled the girl to come forward and hide behind the stone. As Calandra helped her into position, she caught a glance at the girl's face, terrified and eyes wide open. Calandra tried to smile but it was forced and obvious. And my cold hands probably don't help either, she thought.

There was much commotion coming from the room next door and Calandra heard the door begin to open. Swiftly and quietly she closed the store cupboard door. Hop, hop, hop. She never got used to that sound. She heard at least three sets of flippers and waited until she was sure they were going down the corridor. Then, gingerly, she opened the door a touch. It was a party of three and they were just about visible in the gloom of the corridor. Two wore habits such as Calandra was wearing herself, but the other wore an outfit she remembered only too well. Her hand reached over her mouth to suppress a gasp.

The last time she had seen that garb, Churchy had been firing arrows at the wearer. High above the sea on a platform, surrounded by chanting frog- and fish-men, Indy had worn that smock when he had summoned and then banished Dagon. It was a special outfit, made for summoning, made for bringing darkness to a world. Calandra was permanently cold and her skin was like ice but now she felt a shiver. Not again, she thought.

Once she had seen the party ascend the stairs, she motioned to the girl to stay hidden and went by herself to the other room. On opening the door, she was confronted by pictures and murals of Dagon and Mother Hydra, frog- and fish-men, devastation and squalor. Calandra tried not to focus too hard on any picture but she felt the heaviness come and then the tears. Stop trembling, she rebuked herself, and her mind recalled Havers falling into that rabid crowd of hooded amphibians.

Come on, girl, come on, this isn't helping. Check the room, check for anything useful, that's why you came in. Have a look.

There was a desk, mouldy and full of woodworm, on top of which were some old manuscripts and a worn leather book. None of the writing made any sense to Calandra but she recognized Dagon in some of the pictures. She stuffed the loose sheets inside the book and secreted it inside her jacket.

As she carried out a last scan for something useful, Calandra heard that dreaded sound again. Hop, hop, hop. At least it was only a single set of flippers. Calandra drew her broken staff, held a piece in each hand and placed herself behind the door, just out of reach of its arc. Before, the fighting had been chaotic and she had run on instinct, but this was different. And that song ran though her head. Something about the waiting being the hardest part. Hop, hop, hop. The door swung open and a hooded figure entered the room with a single leap.

Calandra brought both sticks down on its head and then followed up with ten more blows at pace. Its legs buckled and it tumbled to the ground. Calandra dragged the prone body to the corner of the room. It was time to move again. She would be stuck here if a crowd came. Returning to the store room, she took the girl by the hand and led her into the corridor. Then she heard it again. Hop, hop, hop. From the far end of the corridor. Hell, no. Quickly Calandra ducked into the main room with the girl and shut the door silently. Hop, hop, hop. There were at least five different hops, she reckoned. Damn.

Calandra looked around the room for any other way out. There was only one lit candle providing the light and the corners were in shadow. Pocketing her sticks, she began tracing the walls with her hands. No one would build a dead end in their main office, especially if they were holding anything precious. There must be a way out. Please God, there must be.

The girl joined her search but on the other side of the room. Hands slid over moist walls and Calandra felt a fungus under her hands. Hop, hop, hop. Halfway down the corridor now. Come on girl, look, Cally, look. It wasn't the initial struggle that worried her. Five of them in a tight space; she could work that and only have to take on at most two at a time. It was the warning they would shout to the rest. Or maybe it was already too late. Maybe they had found the dead hydra. Focus, Cally, focus.

Hop, hop, hop. It was nearly outside now. The girl grunted at Calandra. Turning, she saw the girl pointing at a section of the wall. Calandra ran over and pushed the girl aside. There was a loose stone. Hop, hop, hop. Right outside now. One brick came free. Then another. Move, Cally, move! Dammit, it's not fast enough. Hop, hop, hop. Calandra took her sticks and began to beat the wall; large chunks fell apart. Beyond, she could see a small chamber, reminiscent of a priest-hole. The door started to swing open.

Calandra jammed her staff together and spun it hard before driving the white-hot end into the wall. Brickwork shattered as chunks of wall flew into the room. The girl cowered behind

Calandra and saw a figure in a habit hop into the room with its webbed feet. But Calandra saw a gap in the wall, grabbed the girl's habit and hauled her towards the possible escape. There was a single hole, just about wide enough for a frog-man, and therefore quite a generous space for a human woman.

The girl looked in horror at Calandra who just pointed at the hole as she turned to face the intruders. Without looking back she hammered her staff at the first frog-man, sending him crashing into the far wall. With the other end of her staff she flicked the door back onto the rest of the intruders, slamming it hard in their faces. As they pushed the door back open, she drilled each in turn with the white-hot end of her staff. From behind she heard a dull splashing sound and turned back to the hole to see that the girl had disappeared.

With one last flurry she battered the few frog-men who were still standing. And then she heard a truly dreadful sound. There was wild croaking and a noise like hundreds of wet flannels being slapped all at once. The horde had been alerted and was coming. Time to go, Cally, old girl. Calandra ran and leapt onto the edge of the hole then wrapped her legs around her staff, allowing it to poke out just below her feet. Let's hope it's not too deep, she thought. And she jumped.

The Winged Beast

C alandra splashed into a fast-moving body of water and instantly felt herself being pulled under. Damn, she thought, if they follow us down here then they'll have a ridiculous advantage. Her hair trailed out behind her and she kept her staff pointing just beyond her feet, hoping it would catch any rocks before she slammed into them. But from the force of the water, she believed herself to be in the middle of the flow.

At first all thoughts were about self-preservation, but soon her mind wondered about the fate of the girl who had jumped before her. The poor thing was only wearing a robe and would freeze in this water. Calandra's head bobbed above the surface and she grabbed a breath before being pulled back into the current. The water weaved this way and that before she found herself propelled outwards and down in a waterfall.

There was no way to check what was happening, no reverse gear to pull, so Calandra tried to relax as she fell. Without warning, she crashed into another body of water but this time she was able to rise gently to the surface. The current was weak and when her eyes opened she was surprised to see shafts of daylight. Calandra was floating in a large pool into which the waterfall emptied. It was in a cavern with holes littering its roof, allowing the light to come in. Across the pool was a ledge in the rock just above the waterline and here was sitting the girl, soaked through.

Putting her staff between her legs, Calandra swam over to the ledge. After she had pulled herself up onto the exposed rock, she studied the girl closely. The girl sat huddled with her arms wrapped round her legs and was obviously cold and frightened. I'll need to do something or she'll die from exposure, thought Calandra.

"Come on, girl, let's see if we can wring this out," she said. The girl looked up but didn't move. "Up. Stand up, and we'll dry your clothes." There was no recognition. Damn. Calandra tried all the languages she knew but still there was no response. This was going to be awkward.

Calandra took hold of the girl's arms and stood her upright. Calandra pulled the grey habit off the girl and stripped her of her jacket and half-robe, now just a sarong. Calandra was surprised by how submissive the girl was, standing there naked and failing to cover herself up. She was shivering and a wave of pity flooded through Calandra. She squeezed the water from the sarong and jacket as best she could, discarded the habit and then redressed the girl with the sarong and jacket. Finally, Calandra zipped up the jacket, covering the girl's cleavage.

"Well, girl, the skirt's not the most conservative but at least you don't look like a hooker." The girl looked at her with forlorn eyes. "Now then, how do we get out of here?" Calandra's clothes were wet through but she felt no cold. Or rather, she felt only the same cold she had felt ever since the witch had cursed her eight hundred years ago.

I wish the boys were here, she thought. Not that we women won't manage, but I am a bit stretched for ideas. Havers was always the one for the plans but... well, he won't be making many more. A tear welled in Calandra's duct but froze. She flicked the ice out. Yes, I wish the boys were here. Actually, I bet they would too, she laughed to herself as she looked down at her cold, wet figure. Yeah, they'd love it.

The thought of frog-men following her made her snap out of her longing for the boys. It was time to move, but where? She was surprised that the frog-men hadn't followed her down the drop and into the water. At least, she assumed they hadn't, for she hadn't seen or heard any. There was a narrow staircase cut into the rock and Calandra decided to follow it rather than jump back into the water. Turning to the girl, she signalled her to follow. On reaching the first step, Calandra heard footsteps behind her.

The staircase cut into the wall and the way became dark. The steps were large for a human, but again perfectly sized for a hopping frog. Calandra heard the girl stumble behind her several times but kept her focus ahead into the pitch black, tapping her way forward with her staff.

The steps gave way to a larger space and Calandra felt around the wall in the dark, locating a wooden torch. Checking the girl was standing well back, Calandra swung her staff to a white heat and lit the torch. With the new light, Calandra found another torch, lit it and passed it to the girl, who pulled it close to her, embracing its heat. Meanwhile Calandra explored the room they had entered.

There were shelves of manuscripts up to eight feet high all around the room. At the centre was a large dish with some bones residing at the bottom. This must be some sort of library, thought Calandra, but well hidden. This stuff must be important. She pulled out a book and looked at the symbols on the page. It meant nothing to her. Where was Indy when you needed him?

Quickly she tried various books and manuscripts but all were gobbledygook to her. Realizing there was nothing more to be gained from further investigation, Calandra searched the room for an exit. There was nothing, only the way they had come in. The girl wasn't going to like what Calandra was going to suggest next.

With Calandra leading the way out, the pair made their way back down the steps to the rock ledge. Calandra scanned the cavern but saw no movement. She led the girl to the water's edge and with a variety of hand signals tried to explain the next step of jumping back into the river. At first the girl looked dumb but then she began to shake her head violently. I haven't got time for this thought, Calandra. Grabbing the girl with one hand, she pulled them both back into the water.

The river was less wild than it had been upstream and Calandra was able to hold the girl and her staff as they drifted along. All along the route, little shafts of daylight lit up the way and if you were able to ignore the cold, like Calandra could, the journey was rather pleasant, almost like a dull theme park ride. At one point they could hear the sounds of the street just above them. Wagons rolling, people calling out at each other, trades being advertised. But the sides of the cavern were sheer and there was no way they could climb up to the noises above.

We must have been in the water for at least thirty minutes, thought Calandra. It's a wonder the girl hasn't passed out from the cold. But then she realized that the river wasn't cold. Calandra wasn't as sensitive to temperature differences as other people, at least not since her curse, and it took time for her body to pick up on the rising temperatures. But now the water was more like a hot bath and she couldn't fail to notice.

Especially as a steamy vapour began to rise and then condense on the roof of the extended cavern.

Then there was darkness. The holes in the roof that had been providing the light were behind them but Calandra, still holding the girl, drifted on in darkness. The water was still warm, but without light it was hard to gauge time and Calandra was unsure how long they had sailed in the water before she saw some firelight ahead.

Another cavern appeared, lit up by the cavern walls. But this time they weren't rough walls of rock but solid vast blocks of stone. Cyclopean, that's the word Indy always uses, thought Calandra. She could see movement ahead and so swam as best she could towards the edge of the river, staying in the dark shadows. She felt the girl huddle close to her. Above the lapping of the water on the edges of the cavern, Calandra could hear hopping sounds and that unintelligible croaking those things made.

From her position, Calandra counted five frog-men. Well, four actually; one was definitely a frog-woman. Hussy, thought Calandra, she's barely covered. Although the frog-men don't seem to be taking an interest. I hope I don't end up like that, she mused, all there and no one interested.

The frog-men were on the opposite side of the water from her and were on a substantial platform built alongside the river. It was made of solid rock and looked as if a boat could moor alongside. Glancing further downstream, Calandra saw that the river seemed to end against a far rock face. Damn, she thought, if it flows on it's probably underground. Who knows how long we'd have to hold our breath. Guess it's good for frog-men though. Time to sit and wait.

For an age, Calandra kept them both in the water, waiting

for a chance to mount the stone platform. First, two frog-men left, followed by another one. Then she had to watch as frog-man and frog-woman mated. That was probably the correct technical term but hell, she didn't want to see that again. Eventually the two lovers left and Calandra took the chance to swim to the platform.

Cautiously, she clambered onto the jetty and scanned around. There were three exits, all open spaces cut into the vast stone block that made up the wall behind the platform. The first two were dark inside but the third passageway was lit. From her position in the water, it had been hard to see where the frog-men had exited but she was sure this passage was it. It had light at least; she didn't fancy trying to fight in the dark.

With the girl following her, she tiptoed her way along the stone corridor that led from the third exit. Calandra was aware that although she was making little noise, the girl wasn't as quiet. The corridor led up without steps, its gradient becoming gradually steeper. The walls were damp and warm and to Calandra the air was akin to a tropical garden. After some five minutes, the corridor broke off into four different paths. Three of the paths seemed to stay on the same level but one started with an obvious uphill track.

Calandra and the girl quickly took the uphill track as they heard some hopping sounds close by. The corridor ran sharply uphill before turning abruptly right. Then it broke out into a vast room. But the room wasn't empty.

Calandra only had a few seconds to survey the room. She saw a winged beast on her right side. It had a head similar to that of an eagle, complete with large beak, but the body extended into something more like a salamander. Well, except for the wings. Unlike the creatures the boys had mentioned in Dillingham, this was obviously one complete beast, but one Calandra had never seen before. It seemed docile. There were a few other beasts in the room. Looking up, there was no roof to the vast expanse.

Any further information was lost as a shout broke the air. It wasn't a frog-man croak but a humanoid voice. The language was lost on Calandra, but the presence of a sixty-strong posse over where the voice had originated from wasn't.

Calandra went to turn back to the corridor but the girl grabbed her arm and ran towards the winged beast. Calandra clocked the leather saddle atop the creature and saw that the girl suddenly seemed enlivened. On reaching the beast, the girl ran up the side of the creature, picking out the bones underneath the skin which ran up its side. Quickly the girl climbed into the saddle and grabbed some loose reins. The posse of humanoids had drawn closer and Calandra saw they were in full battle armour, consisting of leather smocks and gauntlets, and carried various pikes and swords.

The winged creature was responding slowly to the girl's encouragement and Calandra decided she needed to buy her some time. Turning to face the oncoming group of soldiers, she let her wings expand and drew pleasure from the gasps of shock. With a body that spoke of every dream and wings and a staff that promised a nightmare, she had broken their confident charge. Come on lads, let's see you handle an old woman!

The first line of five soldiers broke at her, yelling and waving their weapons. Calandra turned sideways and swept two aside with her wing. The first that arrived in front of her took a blow to the head that floored him completely. Calandra didn't wait but bore down on the next attacker, drove her staff into his groin and then lashed out with a foot at the fifth attacker, catching him on the jaw and dropping him instantly. Come on boys, there's more where that came from.

Then Calandra felt the beat of wings behind her and, glancing back, saw that the creature was up on its legs and the girl was waving at her to join them. The second wave of soldiers attacked and Calandra swept her wings into them before running to the winged beast. As the beast became airborne, Calandra jumped and with the aid of her wings glided onto the back of the creature. The creature seemed to struggle with the additional weight and began to circle the room at a low level to gain some momentum.

This meant coming close to the soldiers and the other creatures in the room. A few of the soldiers jumped and secured themselves onto the winged beast. Calandra fought to keep her balance as she moved towards the new arrivals. With her wings outstretched, she was able to reach the soldiers and thrash them with her staff, knocking them to the ground. The creature, freed from this weight, began to rise up in a circular motion and Calandra allowed her wings to vanish lest they get caught in the mounting airflow.

As the beast rose higher, Calandra could see various devices being readied on the ground below. Crossbows of different sizes were loaded and fired at the escaping threesome, but the creature was circling at speed now and most missed their target. The few small bolts that hit the creature were too dainty to penetrate its thick hide. The room was incredibly high and it took a good minute to reach the open roof where a grey day greeted the animal aviators. Below, the soldiers readied a large wooden crossbow that looked more like a siege weapon. As the beast started to clear the top of the room, the bolt was launched. It flew high and struck the beast's side. The creature rocked sideways; Calandra stumbled on its back and lost her footing. She slid down its body and managed to find faint purchase on the start of its tail, but the creature was struggling and clipped the edge of the top of the room. Beyond the room Calandra could see a vast complex surrounded by woodland. But striking the edge had hurt the creature and it reared. It flicked its tail, throwing Calandra aside, and she landed on a nearby rooftop. After rolling to a halt, she watched the beast limping in flight as it cleared the structure she was now on before beginning a descent to the ground. Calandra was stranded atop the structure.

Enter the Dragon

With a flagon of water in one hand, Kirkgordon was propping himself up with his other. He was sitting on some sacks in a dusty storehouse watching the monoped Kilon attend to Nefol. Lying beside the girl was a slumbering Austerley. They were safe, safe from the dark beacon that was Austerley's foot, but he knew this rescue attempt was in a right mess. Austerley was an amputee once again and his mobility, never great to begin with, was further reduced. Havers and Calandra hadn't been seen and the rescue of Alana didn't seem any closer.

Kirkgordon stared at an awakening Nefol, his only bright light in a darkening world. The girl was groggy but at least she was alive, thanks to Kilon's attentions. Of their little group, she was the hardest for him to connect with but to see her moving again brought a lot of joy. He was almost desperate for that dismissive teenage stare she always gave him.

Glancing at the storehouse door, a thick wooden structure with a large crossbeam securing it, Kirkgordon saw the figure in the dark shadows. He had stood behind bulletproof windows, armed guards and fanatical converts, but never had he been guarded by a bogeyman. What was more disturbing was the fact that he appeared to be one of the good guys. This shouldn't be pondered on. A striding Nefol brought him to his senses.

"Where's Calandra? And Havers? Why aren't they here?"

"Easy, girl. They're not here."

"Well, I can see that." And there was the tutting noise. "What have you done with them?"

"I didn't do anything with them. They went to look for someone to help you and they haven't been seen since." Nefol's face fell. "We had to run from our digs, due to Austerley's foot, which as you can see is no more. We couldn't warn them and we haven't heard from them. Kilon, our single-footed friend, hasn't been able to discover their whereabouts."

"Are they dead then?" asked Nefol, eyes welling up.

"I don't know anything, Nefol. Sorry, that's all I got."

"Well, it's not enough. We should go look for them."

"We will, but not now. It's still dark. These streets aren't good in the daylight, never mind at night."

"So I'm expected to just calm down and sit it out till morning?"

"Pretty much. And get some food. You've missed a few meals." Nefol paced off and casually struck a beam with her hand. The wood vibrated and a crack was left behind.

"The Professor is stirring, Archer," said Kilon, "I will try to find him a crutch to assist his walking. He may not think his new-found freedom a great compensation for the lack of a foot. Although I seem to manage on only the one."

Kirkgordon watched Austerley come to and gradually pull himself into a upright position. At first he looked distant, almost contemplative, but then he let loose.

"You said you wouldn't let anyone cut my foot off. You said you wouldn't let them. Look at me, just look at me."

"Piss off, Indy! Just piss right off. Your damned foot nearly got us all killed. Bogey did us all a favour."

"But that was my foot!"

"And your bloody foot attacked me. That stuff in it, that blackness, it got into my head, Indy. It got right in. So don't you even begin to have a go. You brought it all on yourself, taking that girl's foot. I've got two of my team missing, one recovering and I'm stuck in the arse-end, no offence Kilon, of some city in the back of beyond wondering what the hell to do, so Indy take a hint and just piss off!"

Austerley turned away. Nefol stood up against one of the stanchions of the storehouse, eyes gazing at the floor. Kirkgordon drank some more of his water. And the bogeyman lurked in the shadows by the door. There was a silence throughout the storeroom except for the distant, quiet splat of Kilon on the move.

Then came a knock on the door. Nefol and Kirkgordon exchanged glances and then each put a hand on their weapon of choice.

Another knock.

"Kindly open the door, Mr Kirkgordon. We have much to discuss and not much time to decide on your course of action." The voice had all the qualities of Havers except for one thing: instead of a brisk tone of command, there was the slightest sneer, the element of delight in coercion. Kirkgordon loaded and then drew his bow.

"Bogey, open the door and let him in."

The door was opened slowly by a seemingly invisible hand. From out of the shadows of night hobbled Farthington. Dressed in a dapper suit and wearing an eye patch, he was in obvious pain as he took centre stage in the room.

"Not looking so healthy these days, Farthington," said Kirkgordon.

"Indeed, Mr Kirkgordon, but then neither is Mr Austerley or yourself. I see he has rid himself of the blackness. It was quite unsavoury, turned that young girl at Dillingham into a drooling well of evil. Still, at least she had a saviour. Quite a sacrifice from the old priest." Nefol's hand tensed on her staff.

"That's enough of the goading, Farthington. State your business before my patience disappears."

"Business? Well, I believe my business is now your business. It appears we are now fugitives from the same enemy."

"Maybe Austerley and you. But not me, Havers," spat Kirkgordon. "You're my enemy. As long as you have my wife, you're my enemy."

"Then let's work out a solution to that. A mutual accommodation. You may have heard that Dagon wasn't too happy at being put back into his cage and has been seeking myself and Mr Austerley. Unfortunately, my travel between our world and this one through the portal in Russia has come to the attention of his agents, and I believe that they now intend to manifest Dagon right here in this city. This would have obviously catastrophic effects for this dear little place and I doubt it would stop there. Once in this place he could use the portal and take command in our world, Mr Kirkgordon. I'm sure neither you nor I would relish such an invasion."

"Churchy," interrupted Austerley, "we need to close the portal. We need to leave and get back now."

"Not without Calandra," shouted Nefol.

"And not without my wife," said Kirkgordon. "And what of Kilon's world, Indy? He's helped us and so we just abandon him? One thing bothers me, Farthington. You know Dagon's coming here, so why haven't you just popped back home and closed the portal yourself?"

"Because, my good man, I didn't open it. And that means I cannot close it, or I would have done exactly as you suggested. I'm afraid only the person who opened a portal such as that would be able to close it. Wouldn't that be so, Mr Austerley?"

Austerley hung his head.

"You opened that portal?" said Kirkgordon. "Bloody hell, Austerley, you really do stick your nose into the trough, don't you?"

"In defence of the Professor," said Kilon, entering into the fray from the back of the room, "it was how my family and I returned home. Although we never knew it was you, we did suspect and searched for you in our world for some time."

"You've been here before, Indy?" asked Kirkgordon.

"No. Never. I did open the door but I never went through. When I tried to test it, it seemed unstable. It was only when I saw how Farthington and his lackeys used it that I understood it to be safe enough."

"And you never thought you should mention any of this?"

"Well, with Havers around one doesn't mention any sloppy work. He's not very forgiving." Kirkgordon, mouth wide open, stared at Austerley. "What Indy, what?" Kirkgordon just shook his head.

"So you have a choice, Mr Kirkgordon. Will you tuck tail and flee or will you stand here and stop them from bringing Dagon to this place?" Farthington, one eye covered by the patch, stared intently with his other eye.

"We are not leaving Calandra!" insisted Nefol.

"No, Nefol, we aren't," said Kirkgordon. "We won't be leaving anyone behind. And we won't abandon Kilon and Bogey to their fate either."

"Churchy, think about this. This is Dagon we are talking

about," said Austerley, rising up onto his good leg. "We won't just die, we'll end up in a perpetual darkness, soul shredded forever. Do you even begin to understand what I'm saying?"

"No, Indy. I really don't. But I won't be able to live with myself if we abandon Cally and Havers, if we leave Kilon and Bogey and everyone else in this place to what you have just described. And I am not leaving without Alana. So here's the plan. We are going to stop this summoning of Dagon, we are going to get everyone back to their proper worlds and then Indy is going to clean up his mess and close the damn portal. And I will beat the tripe out of anyone who doesn't lend their full weight to this."

"Oh, well said, Mr Kirkgordon, well said," sneered Farthington. "Such ambition. And I wish you bonne chance."

"And you, Farthington, you smug bastard, are coming with us!"

"And pray, Mr Kirkgordon, what makes you think I will be accompanying you on whatever plan you are hatching?"

"Because you are here. You have sought me out. We've been on your trail and you knew we would come. You had the upper hand holding Alana and the smart move was to stay hidden and keep your joker. Instead you are here, which means that you can't stop Dagon and trust me, if you don't come with me, I'll kill you here. I'm done with games, Farthington. You need me and so it's my terms. And that means I need you."

"And pray what help can I be?"

"We're blind when it comes to this place. Yes, Kilon can help us somewhat but you've been dealing with Dagon and his followers so you have the inside scoop. That means you're useful. And I know you can fight when you have to. So you're in."

"Very good, Mr Kirkgordon, but where do we start? What is it that I can do for you?"

"You have contacts here. You know that his followers are here and I dare say you can get us a lead onto them. Indy, do you know how they would summon him here?"

"It's not so much summon as invite." Austerley gulped at Kirkgordon's angry stare. "But as you say summon, eh... no."

"Then we need to know how. Farthington, you need to get us that lead. You have twelve hours. Until then we have a truce. If I don't hear from you, all bets are off."

"Very good, Mr Kirkgordon."

"Oh, and Farthington, if Alana is hurt in any way, I will come for you."

"I expect no less. Twelve hours, Mr Kirkgordon. I will be in touch." With a smart turn on his heels, Farthington made his way back out the door.

"I'm glad you decided not to kill him right here," said a deep voice from the shadows.

"Why's that, Bogey?" asked Kirkgordon.

"Well the fifty or so guards outside the door may have had something to say about it. He's connected, Archer, right to the top in this city."

"If that's so, why doesn't he just get his contacts to get rid of this Dagon threat?"

"Because nobody touches them. Wherever they have been people have left them alone. The consequences are too dire to think about. Madness generally ensues."

"Well it's good he's come onto our side, because madness seems to be the pre-requisite. That right, Indy?" Austerley grunted and began to hop off.

"Professor, before you go anywhere I think I may have

something to interest you," said Kilon, producing a wooden leg. "It wasn't easy to get on such short notice but I think it should fit okay, although the transition can be sore, others have said."

"I guess it will have to do if I am going to be entering the fray again," spat Austerley.

"Easy, Indy," said Kirkgordon. "Thanks Kilon, it's much appreciated, as is all this. I may have seemed uneasy at your appearance but you have a very kind disposition."

"You are welcome, Archer. And thank you for volunteering to save my city. Many wouldn't."

Kirkgordon lay back down and tried to rest up but his mind was racing. What threat was this that Farthington had reached out to him? What had a place like this so scared that they wouldn't deal with the frog-men? I don't feel lost at sea, more like drowning in the depths. And my two wise heads are missing, dammit. His mind shot back to the blackness covering him and the depression that had come. This had to be stood up to, just like the priest had stood up. This was his purpose.

"Why did you deal with him?" Nefol was standing over him.

"What would you have done?" asked Kirkgordon, tapping the sack beside him for Nefol to sit on.

"I wanted to kill him. I wanted to batter him first and then hang his body up so that he screamed in pain."

"I get that. Trust me, Nefol, I do get that, but it wouldn't be helpful."

"Maybe not, but I would feel better knowing he was dead."

"No you wouldn't. You're too young to have so much hate... actually you're not, especially after all that you've seen. And now that Calandra's missing. But it changes nothing. You won't feel better when Farthington's dead."

"And why not? He practically had a go at my father's sacrifice."

"Yes, he did. And he is full of evil and hate. If you kill him for revenge then you'll just open yourself up to the same hate. Your father is dead and it hurts. But nothing you do to other people will change that. Healing will only come from within you. And from Him."

"But you don't get on well with God, do you?" asked Nefol.

"Well, it's not been a perfect relationship lately. But trust me, or rather trust Him, revenge will bring nothing to you. You'll end up like Havers. Talented and brave but mistrustful, manipulative and full of hate. Don't trust his outer demeanour; he's broken inside. You're not yet. Whether you stay that way is up to you and no one else. Take your father's example: sacrifice and trust, it's what we all need."

"Bullshit, Churchy, bullshit," shouted Austerley from across the room. "You need to take what you can, and when and if you can stop these things then you do it. No mercy for those that tried to kill me."

"We need Farthington at the moment. But it's up to you, Nefol. Take Long John's advice or mine. But beware vengeance. It never healed anything."

Leaving Town

Standing atop the highest city wall, Kirkgordon surveyed the temple cut into the rock. Although he had passed it on his journey into the city, now in the morning's dim light its vastness was impressive even at this distance. But there was a stillness about it. Nothing seemed to enter it and nothing had come out of it in the three hours he had been watching.

"How good is your source?" asked Kirkgordon.

"Really, there's no need to be vulgar. If the information wasn't solid, I wouldn't have brought it to you. You really need to develop some trust, Mr Kirkgordon, if we are going to be working together."

"Farthington, that is an unknown and some distance away. If we are going there then we need to be sure."

"The source is good. Mr Havers was moved to that location during the night. Apparently he wasn't in a good state of repair either."

"And you're sure they were frog-men."

"They hop, Mr Kirkgordon, it really isn't that difficult to identify them. Give my people some credit."

Kirkgordon pulled the rudimentary binoculars from his eyes and thought hard. Havers wasn't that easy to catch. There must be plenty of them.

"Are we going to stay here and stare?" asked Farthington.

"Nothing about Calandra. Are you sure about that? She wouldn't leave him."

"Maybe she didn't have a choice. She seems capable of making the tough calls." Kirkgordon ignored the jibe.

"Okay, we move out in an hour. Austerley, Nefol, me, you and the bogeyman."

"And Hanwere, my associate," added Farthington.

"Who?"

"Hanwere, my guard. Takes care of me on my travels, Mr Kirkgordon. You should get one. Or maybe you already have one. Or at least had. Miss Calandra is much better looking, I'll give you that. Is she a bodyguard or a personal assistant?"

Kirkgordon planted a punch right onto Farthington's chin, flooring the dragon and bringing a man clad in black running towards him. Squaring up, Kirkgordon looked into the newcomer's eyes and drew his bow in anticipation. The man wore a hood covering his face but on reaching the scene he dropped it and revealed the face of a lizard. Kirkgordon just stared on, no longer surprised by the visage of anyone he met.

"No, Hanwere, stand down. That was deserved. My apologies, Mr Kirkgordon," said Farthington, standing and rubbing his chin. "Not a moment's hesitation. This does bode well for our journey."

"You can have your gimp, Farthington, but make sure he's on a tight leash." Farthington nodded and strode away to make final preparations for departure. Austerley, who had been watching from a distance, now came half-limping and half-hopping over.

"So what's the deal, Churchy?"

"They took Havers there. Frog-men, according to Farthington."

"I don't trust him, Churchy."

"And I do? Give me some credit, Indy."

"Then where's Alana?"

"She's missing."

"Did he say that?" asked Austerley.

"No, he didn't have to. If he had her he would have shown her to me to get me on board, then shown me what would happen if I failed on this trip. He doesn't have her. I think the frog-men do. Anyone else and he would have said. Or rather, he would have sorted it out with his connections. But as Bogey said, no one goes near the frog-men."

"Well, if they are taking Havers there..."

"Then there's a good chance Alana is there too," finished Kirkgordon. "And Cally is missing, Indy. I'm sorry, but this thing just got so much bigger. It was meant to be a rescue mission but now it's like being back on the island."

"Two worlds this time, though. Look, Churchy, last time I knew all the rituals and the methods. This time I don't. I can't just jump in."

"I know, but if there's anything written about it, I need you to read it. This won't get done without you, Indy. Without you, there's no life for any of us when he comes through whatever portal they dream up. Even Farthington needs you this time."

"Still don't trust him." Austerley bent down and rubbed at his stump where it joined the false piece of leg. "I don't know what pace I can keep. You know I'll slow you down."

"Look, Indy," said Kirkgordon, "I know you'll be slow and probably make us more of a target. I've already asked Kilon to stay behind because of his lack of speed. But you I need, however much you drag us down. I'll keep you safe, just like in Russia. We have Nefol too. Just focus on your job. I need to understand what is going to happen, stop it, and then get everyone, including Alana, safely back to our world."

"What about Farthington?"

"I couldn't give a damn about Farthington if we get the rest done."

"Havers won't see it like that."

"Havers has enough on his plate. He needs to start worrying about himself and not the bigger picture for once. Come on, Long John, let's go."

An hour later the small party were on the road, Nefol and Hanwere on point, Austerley escorted by Kirkgordon in the middle and Farthington bringing up the rear. Kirkgordon hoped that their approach would be hidden by the immense canopy of trees that surrounded the city, but deep down he didn't truly believe it.

His mind was also distracted once again by the two foremost women in his life. Alana would swing out of his unconscious mind into scenarios where she was being abused or even killed. Fighting hard to push such images from his internal vista, he found Calandra appearing, swinging upside down as he had found her on the island. Most disturbing was how he would begin to process the demise of either party and then set about planning life with the other. He needed some action.

Progress was slower than desired due to Austerley's awkwardness with his new appendage. He would clump along, failing to achieve any regular rhythm, and had fallen several times. It was getting to the point that Kirkgordon felt the pain of carrying the professor over his shoulder might be worth it. There was also the other tick that kept ruffling through the back of his mind. Where was Bogey?

Kirkgordon had estimated it would take a good four to five hours at Austerley's pace and the party was just over the halfway mark when Nefol signalled from up ahead. The casual onlooker would not have noticed the difference in her demeanour but Kirkgordon spotted it immediately.

"Indy," whispered Kirkgordon, "stay close."

"Why, what's up?

"I don't know, but stay close." Kirkgordon scanned the vegetation around him for something different or unusual. Despite his missing eye, Farthington instantly spotted the change in the archer and smartly increased his pace to come alongside him.

"What is the issue, Mr Kirkgordon?"

"Something is out there, Farthington. Nefol has seen something but I can't see it yet."

"Are you sure? Hanwere hasn't seen anything and he has more experience than the priest's daughter."

"Don't underestimate her. Keep a good lookout."

"Always, Mr Kirkgordon, always." Farthington dropped back and Kirkgordon tried to watch where Nefol was looking. As he was behind her, he looked for the tell-tale turn of her head. None was forthcoming. Damn, she was good.

From the forest beside him, Kirkgordon saw a dark shape move and then a figure was tossed face down onto the road. Nefol and Hanwere both turned on the sound and had weapons at the creature's throat.

"Been tailing us for at least the last half hour," came a deep voice from the dark of the forest. Kirkgordon turned the figure over and saw the face of a frog-man, its eyes frozen wide open and its mouth gaping. Kirkgordon slapped its face and tried to find some sign of life but the figure remained motionless.

Bloody hell, he thought, it looks scared to death. I guess he really is a bogeyman.

"Amazing how they can sneak around with those webbed feet," commented Farthington. "Rather ingenious creatures, really."

Austerley whirled round on him and placed a finger firmly on his chest. "You worked with those bastards. They set a family up like a horror show. There's nothing ingenious about them, just plain sick."

"My, my, Mr Austerley, how your views change like the wind."

Austerley swung a punch which Farthington easily avoided. The unexpected follow-through caught Austerley off balance and he fell to the ground. At first he let out a low grunt but then he grabbed Farthington's leg and began to bite him. Hanwere raced forward and gave Austerley a low punch in the back, forcing him to release the bite and cry out. The lizard then felt Nefol's staff across his chest and he was flung to the side. He rolled back up, ready for the next attack.

"Enough!"

Everyone stared at Kirkgordon, who had drawn his bow and was aiming it in turn around the four individuals. There was silence amongst the group as each breathed heavily.

"Nefol, get Austerley up. Farthington, stand Hanwere down. I think we all know what we think of each other, so as of now there will be no talk that isn't relevant to our mission. Am I understood?" Kirkgordon's bow remained drawn. "I need you vigilant, not fighting each other."

"Then I suggest I take point with Hanwere and Miss Nefol can walk the rear with Mr Austerley."

"No, Farthington. I put you where I need you. There we stay.

I think there will be enough enemies to fight without renewing old battles. If they had a scout on us, they know we're coming. Dagon's shadow is on us, all of us. So forget the past or there won't be a future."

"Well said, Archer." The voice was low and from the shadows. And now my top ally and supporter is a bogeyman, thought Kirkgordon. That's one to tell the kids. Wonder how they're holding up with Alana's sister. I'm telling myself they're resilient but some things are too much. But look at Nefol. She's busted up inside and yet she fights like a pro.

The journey continued until they reached the end of the tree cover. At this point, Kirkgordon ordered them to break off into the long grass cover as he took a spyglass from Farthington and surveyed the building.

"I can't see anything. Did you, Farthington?"

"Indeed not, Mr Kirkgordon. Quite at a loss for a door."

"Give me that," said Austerley, grabbing the glass from Kirkgordon. He stood taking in the building for some five minutes, rebutting any questions about how he was doing. A short bout of low-level muttering followed before Austerley sat down and closed his eyes. Farthington stepped forward to ask a question but Kirkgordon waved him away and took Nefol to one side.

"Listen, I don't trust Farthington one bit but we need to keep a focus on what matters. Number one priority is finding out about how they intend to bring Dagon through to this world and for that we need Austerley. So he is our prime protectee. Whatever else happens, we need to keep him alive and functioning. Second to that are Alana, Cally and Havers. Dealing with Farthington comes at the end, only then. Do you understand?"

Nefol nodded and stared off at the huge building they were hoping to infiltrate. So young, thought Kirkgordon. How is she holding up to all this? Heck, she was nearly dead less than a day ago. But you can see Cally's influence coming through the know-it-all teenager. She didn't even give me a tut.

"Nefol, we will get Cally."

"If she's alive."

"Nefol." Kirkgordon turned her head with his hand and kissed her forehead. "Take it from an old git, she's alive." But he saw such doubt in her eyes. They started to well up and a tear ran down her cheek. Holding her cheeks in both hands, he wiped the tear away with his thumb.

"You need to believe, there's no other way. Focus on the goal, trust they will be there and throw everything at it," Kirkgordon whispered.

"And if they're not?"

"Just trust they will be."

Kirkgordon heard Austerley stand up and hobble over towards him but he continued to hold Nefol's face. He needed to be her Cally just now.

"Churchy," interrupted Austerley, "I think I can do it."

"Kind of a moment here, Indy."

"It's okay," said Nefol. "The old git's got work to do." And she smiled.

"Okay then, Indy, amaze me."

"It isn't obvious to the smaller mind, but if one can open up the realms of belief in one's brain and cross-reference that with even a sparse knowledge of the Elders, one can easily deduce most things, and in this case the mode of infiltration to this domain. Conceptually, I doubt you'll get it, but I believe a man of intelligence would concur—"

"Dammit, Indy, where's the door?"

"Over there." Austerley pointed to an apparently solid piece of stone some fifteen feet up from the ground.

"That's just rock. Where's the door?"

Austerley shook his head. "Sometimes I forget how slow you can be. Who uses the door?"

"The frog-men," answered Nefol.

"Exactly. And if you're a frog-man in a foreign place, where would you put your door?" asked Austerley. Kirkgordon frowned and shrugged his shoulders.

"High up," said Nefol. "Somewhere others can't leap. But where is the door? I can't see anything."

"No, you can't," said Austerley. Kirkgordon threw his hands up in impatience. "I'm getting to it, Churchy," rebuked Austerley. "It can be sensed, if you know how of course. So it's a good thing I'm here as there isn't any other intelligentsia around."

"And you would be dead if we didn't cover your pompous arse. Now just tell me where that pissing door is." Kirkgordon's face looked ready to commit murder if his request wasn't met.

"I did tell you. There!"

"But there's nothing there."

"Yes there is, but you can't see it." Austerley watched Kirkgordon's eyebrows rise. "Trust me, Churchy, it's there. If Calandra drew some chalk lines up there you would jump through them to wherever, so why is it so hard to follow my lead? I am the expert. Churchy, are you listening? Churchy? Churchy!"

But Kirkgordon's eyes had been drawn to a large beast emerging over the top of the vast construction. It had wings and someone, or something, was on top of it. And it was descending rapidly. Kirkgordon estimated its path and shoved Austerley to one side.

"Nefol, watch Austerley and keep out of sight. I'll be back."

The Girl from the Sky

There was an almighty crash as the winged beast fell into the tree canopy. Hurdling over the occasional fallen tree and depressed mound, Kirkgordon raced hard to the scene. When he arrived, several trees had been taken down by the creature, which was lying motionless with its neck at what Kirkgordon perceived to be an awkward angle. The fact it looked like a lizard with a bird's head meant he wasn't too sure what angle anything should be at but it didn't look good.

Scanning the scene, he spotted a girl some twenty metres from the creature, rolling around in some distress. She was wearing Calandra's leather jacket. Kirkgordon also noticed her legs as she flailed about, a loose piece of material failing to cover them in an adequate fashion. Making his way slowly towards her, Kirkgordon drew his bow and swung it around, covering the area surrounding him.

As he drew closer, the girl looked up at him, her eyes widening in terror. Kirkgordon kept the aim of the bow away from her.

"It's okay. I'm not here to hurt you." He put out his hand to her but she crawled backwards, never taking her eyes from him. "That jacket belongs to my friend. Where did you get the jacket?" Kirkgordon's phrasing reminded himself of his ineptness with foreigners and he slowed down his speech like he was talking to an imbecile. He fully expected himself to start shouting at the poor girl in a loud voice.

Kirkgordon pointed repeatedly at the jacket and eventually the girl stood up. Quivering, she started to unzip the top and before Kirkgordon could say anything she was stood topless handing it over to him.

"No, no. I don't want it. I just want to know about it." She probably thinks I'm some sort of pervert. The girl was starting to undress completely and Kirkgordon had to throw her the jacket back to grab her attention. "Get changed, please get changed."

It was then that he heard noises in the distance, thrashing sounds of a pursuer who wasn't interested in sneaking up on its prey. As soon as the girl had zipped the jacket back up, he grabbed her arm but she pulled it away from him and cowered on the ground. The crashing sounds were growing closer.

"Look, I'm sorry, but one day you'll thank me. Although I might not understand the lingo." Kirkgordon dealt the girl a sharp blow to the neck area and she dropped silently to the ground. He slung his bow over one shoulder and picked the girl up and placed her over the other. At least she was lighter than Austerley. Rather than make a direct line back towards his party, Kirkgordon headed away from the temple then circled back round towards the group. He found them secluded in undergrowth beneath a fallen tree which the moss and roots had grown over, leaving a hollow beneath.

"Another scantily clad woman, we might have guessed." Nefol followed up her comment with a scornful look at Kirkgordon before her face broke into a smug smile.

"What's wrong with her?" asked Austerley.

"Had to knock her out. She was petrified. I think she's been a slave of some sort and probably abused. She was terrified of everything. And there were pursuers. Where did they come from?"

"The temple, duh," said Nefol.

"I did kind of guess that, but exactly where?"

"From the door you don't believe exists. Imagine, the much maligned Professor Austerley is correct again," taunted Austerley.

"If I can just interrupt, Mr Kirkgordon," said Farthington. "While your fellow adventurers and yourself argue over your triumphs and disasters, we are being hunted by frog-men who came from that building. And there plenty of them. I suggest our current position is untenable and we should move quickly."

"I take the point, Farthington, but the girl is wearing Calandra's jacket."

"It looks very similar, but how do you know it's hers?" asked Nefol.

"Well, that girl certainly hasn't got the... equipment, shall we say, to fully fill that jacket. I reckon that jacket would hug Cally's figure good and tight, just like she wears it."

"Unbelievable!" said Nefol barely keeping her voice to a hush. "Is the zip the same? Any familiar markings? Arm length? No, none of that, but give Kirkgordon a chest to identify and we're in business." And the tut had returned.

"Sorry. I'm a bloke, it's natural."

"And he's right," said Austerley, "she'd definitely fill that." Nefol shook her head. "What do you reckon, Farthington?" asked Austerley.

"I'm a dragon and not so vulgar. Now, can we move out?"

"No. Cally's definitely in there and this girl knows something.

I think she could be key to finding Cally," said Kirkgordon.

"That and her chest!"

"Enough, Nefol. Indy, I'm going to wake the girl up. She never spoke but she didn't seem to understand English. The only other thing I know is she came down on a flying lizard with a bird's head."

"Hold on," said Austerley, "Like an eagle's head and a salamander body?"

"Well, I guess so."

"It didn't have a chest so he's not so sure."

"Nefol, enough," implored Kirkgordon. I am never telling her what actually happened, he thought. "Are you ready, Indy?"

"I think she's not from round here," said Austerley.

"You mean she's from the city," asked Kirkgordon.

"No," replied Austerley in a derogatory tone, "she's not from this realm or world. The creature is from a place known as Hythoraph, a hot and dry land. Never been there but I have read a lot about it."

"Do you know the language?"

"Not all of them. There are at least five main languages and countless dialects. I know the mother tongues but as for the irregularities, I'm not so proficient."

"Well, give it a go. Ready?"

Austerley nodded and Kirkgordon sat the girl in an upright position. With a sharp strike, again on her neck, Kirkgordon brought the girl around. Her hands shot out and she tried to run. Kirkgordon grabbed her, holding her tight, and placed a firm hand over her mouth.

Austerley began to ask questions in various languages until he saw recognition in her eyes. Kirkgordon felt his impatience rise as the girl still didn't speak but occasionally nodded or shook her head. For at least five minutes Austerley continued to probe her with questions and the rest of the group kept their ears peeled for sounds from beyond their makeshift place of refuge.

"Calandra is in there." Kirkgordon nearly missed the comment. He had wearied of Austerley's foreign interrogation.

"And?" said Kirkgordon.

"And what?"

"Anything else. Whereabouts? Is she fit and healthy? Any other pertinent issues? I mean you were talking for five minutes."

"And maybe you didn't notice, but she said nothing."

"No, but there must be more," answered Kirkgordon, softening his tone a little.

"There are lots of frog-men but there's others too. She didn't know about any portal but she was abused and left at the mercy of a hydra. That's where she met Calandra. Apparently Calandra killed it."

"Most impressive from Miss Calandra, but can we make a move?" asked Farthington.

"Ask the girl if she will come inside and help us find Calandra," ordered Kirkgordon.

The girl recoiled at the suggestion from Austerley and Kirkgordon pondered his next move.

"Ask if she wants to go or stay with us. Tell her we are going in but she can go off on her own or I'll get her back to the city." Austerley nodded and posed the question.

"She wants to go to the city with me."

"Well that's not happening. Tell her we have a friend who'll take her. He's pretty scary but he will protect her."

"I'm not returning to the city, Mr Kirkgordon, and neither is Hanwere," said Farthington.

"No you're not. Bogey is. I wouldn't entrust the girl to you."

It took a while before she agreed and then some time to inform Bogey, who was in the shadows and slightly aloof, but arrangements were made and soon the girl disappeared into the undergrowth surround by a moving shadow. There was still a commotion beneath the tree canopy and the group held their position until Nefol had been sent to scout out the surrounding area. On her return, and with confirmation that there was a little distance between the frog-men and themselves, Kirkgordon gave the all clear to move out.

The Ice Maiden Returns

"Get yourself in gear, girl, who knows what's coming next."

Speaking aloud often calmed the nerves and Calandra knew she needed to ease herself into a thoughtful, rational frame of mind. She pushed down with her arms and sprang up onto her feet. There was a screaming assault from her nervous system, letting her know the extent of the injuries she had sustained, but she pushed them away from her mind, instead concentrating on her next move.

There were faint shouts emanating from the roof exit they had flown through. Swinging round, she couldn't see any sign of the creature or the girl. Best of luck to you, she thought. Now, where am I?

Standing on the flat roof, Calandra could see a parapet surrounding it and made a beeline towards the roof's edge. When she looked over there was a large drop onto other roofs and she thought about jumping. But then she had a feeling that something was missing. Her hand flexed. Where's my staff?

There was nothing close by. Who knows where it might have dropped? Damn. It was like losing your right arm. And maybe your left. Still, there was no time to think about that. The descent off the roof was not available without the staff to ease her fall, so Calandra scanned the rooftop again. There was a small hatch on the far side. Time to move.

The hatch was open and showed a large drop to a granite floor. There was no ladder but then again the froggies wouldn't need one. Nothing for it. Calandra hung down from the opening, lowering herself as close to the ground as she could get, and then dropped down. On landing she rolled sideways to reduce the force, but a stabbing pain shot up her leg. She clutched it tight.

Moving the leg was agony. Clearly something had gone. Through the pain, something else was bothering Calandra. In the far corner of the room she heard a slapping of webbed feet. Large bulbous eyes stared at her from the dark and she could see the tip of an ornate halberd. I'm not in good enough shape for this, she thought.

The eyes suddenly rose in the air and the halberd's deadly point came directly down from above. Years of combat experience kicked in and she rolled clear before the tip struck. Rotating on her hands, she allowed her good leg to kick hard into the frog-man's side, sending him to the floor. The halberd toppled clear and Calandra reached desperately for it. A shadow took to the air and as it fell from above she managed to raise the halberd straight upright. The frog-man fell onto it like a piece of skewered meat and slid down the pole until its eyes were in front of Calandra's face. It exhaled a putrid breath over her, nearly causing her to puke.

With all her strength, she pushed the frog-man away from her and then crawled over to him. He wore a number of leather belts and fixings which Calandra now fought to release. Having freed a number, she began to strap up her leg, paying particular attention to the knee. When complete, she slowly lifted herself upright.

It still hurt like hell but it would do. Now Cally, old girl, what are you going to do? The room had one exit and she knew she needed to hurry. They would be searching for her and she needed a better shelter than this. She took the halberd, green blood still dripping from it, and wiped it dry on the frog-man's body. Then, using it as a walking aid, Calandra made her way to the exit.

The door opened into a dimly lit corridor with large steps descending from it. With her knee strapped, Calandra had to turn herself sideways in order to descend, slowing her progress significantly. But with a little practice it became easier. She was congratulating herself on a wonderful effort when through a patch of broken fabric near her knee she saw that her skin was translucent.

The rest of her body was her normal pale self, as far as she could see, but her knee was turning to ice. And with it, the leg was becoming more manageable. It took her back to that time with Ferrean and the incident. The time when she got her curse. She felt a tear emerge and freeze on its duct. A flick of her eyelashes and it crunched off to the floor. Well, that was some time ago.

She thought about the boys and what they were doing. And then she thought of Nefol. The poor girl had lost her world when her father had been killed by Farthington, burnt alive right in front of her. She had coped amazingly well but inside, Calandra knew Nefol was falling apart. Vengeance was rising up and being here wasn't helping. She needed to get back out for Nefol's sake. The girl needed a mother right now.

She had never thought about children except possibly around Ferrean. She was a warrior after all, and the quiet life didn't find her easily. Churchy was a possibility. A family with him…

but then he already had one. It was no possibility, just a dream. A lustful wish. No, she'd been given a child to take care of and that was where she needed to stay.

There was a sound up ahead. Carefully, Calandra made her way forward, scanning into the gloom. Stood in front of a wooden door in the corridor was a guard, kitted in full armour and holding a pike staff. He hadn't spotted her. Looking at the feet and then the eyes, Calandra deduced the guard was human, or at least not a frog-man. For a moment she wondered how to get past, but then it occurred to her that a guard meant there was something worth protecting and her curiosity got the better of her.

Although she never depended on it, her femininity was something Calandra was more than happy to use if the moment called for it. Leaving the halberd a little way down the corridor, Calandra crawled up to the guard in a fake show of pain. Unmoved, he grabbed her by the hair and pulled her to her feet before shoving her face first into the wall. A rope was tied around her hands and she was pushed towards the door. The guard called out in a language unknown to Calandra but she heard the clanks and knocks of bolts being undone and keys turned.

She was kicked through the door and sprawled to the ground in the centre of a small room. Although the room was dark, she picked out at least four different voices. Without knowing the language she wasn't completely sure of their intent until a hand smacked her backside and gripped it eagerly. Pulled to her feet, she saw four men surveying her with sexual excitement. Although dressed in their armour, they had removed their helmets and one was removing clothing from around his groin area. Really guys, she thought. I was impartial to you, just thought of you as unfortunate soldiers. But now I'm pissed.

One of the guards stepped forward and reached with both hands towards Calandra's chest. Like a mouse trap, she whipped her forehead right into his face, sending him sprawling backwards. Realizing the guards were stunned, Calandra continued forward to deliver a wicked kick to the exposed groin of her presumptive abuser. Another guard stepped up to her and threw a punch which she swerved away from before kicking him hard in the side.

She had lost track of the fourth guard but was quickly appraised of his position as he grabbed her from behind, a large arm choking her and locked tight. The third guard had recovered and punched her hard in the stomach, winding her. Calandra desperately sought air but found none and she felt herself start to weaken. But as she went limp, something else ignited within her. It had been so long since the last time, but she knew immediately what it was.

The guard holding her by the throat felt a burning sensation on his arms where he was contacting Calandra. But it was no fire, rather a cold burn. At the same time his colleague had reached beyond Calandra's clothing to her skin. He also felt his hands burn and tried to retract them, but they refused to leave Calandra's skin, like they were stuck to her.

Calandra looked at the face of her assailant and saw a look of terror. His skin turned white. She couldn't see herself but she knew her own skin was now like ice. The man in front of her froze up like a giant sculpture, his armour cracking with the cold. The arm around her throat snapped off and fell to the floor, shattering on impact. With air returning to her lungs, she pushed with her arms and shoulders and the man in front toppled away from her. There was a crash and he shattered into pieces of ice. She heard the guard behind her break up like a sheet of glass.

Calandra fell to her knees, her head in her hands, feeling the smooth, solid lines of her cheeks. She wanted to cry, wanted to let out her anger at being this way again.

"You bitch! You bitch! You took him from me."

Her tears were frozen and she shuddered with the anger and pain flowing within her. Before her was Ferrean's face, his look of horror at seeing her change, and then his body exploding into a thousand pieces. And that other face in the storm, mocking her and her pain.

Calandra opened her eyes and saw puddles of water around her. The other two guards were fleeing the room. She knew she had to move, had to run, but something caught her eye. There was a mirror on the far wall and despite all common sense telling her not to, she dragged herself to it. When this had happened before it was a time with no mirrors, only reflections in water, and she hadn't seen herself properly.

Her face was like glass but there was a ribbon of granulation running through the middle of her head. Her hair remained dark but had tinges of ice running through it. Her body was taut and muscular as before but now she was translucent. Looking inside her top, her whole body was clear.

And her eyes were blue, sharp and cold. So this is me, she thought. I am the Ice Maiden. They should have kept her locked away, they should never have brought her out. Now they'll pay.

The door opened and two guards ran in. She saw their fear even as they attacked with their swords. With each hand she caught their weapons. A flow of ice ran from her, down their weapons and onto their bodies. They froze and then shattered. Yes, they'll pay.

Into the Temple

Kirkgordon surveyed the sheer wall ahead of him. Even from the thickets it looked impressive, stone rising up vertically. Cyclopean, Austerley would say. Kirkgordon never liked the word as it drew out all Austerley's talk about the Elders. He remembered how the kirk elders in his Scottish church had been talked about with fear, but they had nothing on Austerley's friends.

Still, there was a problem before him. The entire team needed to get through a gap a little larger than a human in size and some fifteen feet up a sheer face. It looked impassable, unclimbable due to the smoothness of the surface. But there was an idea forming in his mind.

"Farthington," said Kirkgordon, "have you got anything that would stick into that rock face?"

The dragon held his face down and shook his head. "It looks like we are a bit stuck, Mr Kirkgordon. I did hope you would be more resourceful than this."

"Now look here—" Kirkgordon felt Nefol tap his shoulder. "Not now Nefol. Farthington, are you telling me—" Another tap on his shoulder. "Nefol, later. Surely your wingman there has got something up his sleeve—"

"Can I get a word—"

"Nefol, enough! We're trying to get a plan together."

There was a tut, distinct and very audible, intended to show great distain. Kirkgordon turned to tell Nefol that this wasn't the time for her nonsense but was forced to duck as the edge of Nefol's staff swung past his head. The staff continued to swing round until the edges blazed white. Kirkgordon was on his knees watching the weapon swirl over his head until at last Nefol let it fly from her grasp. The staff continued spinning until it embedded itself beside the opening Kirkgordon had been examining.

"Now, take one of the rope arrows and we can all get up to it." Nefol finished speaking and stared hard at Kirkgordon.

I can feel her crying out *idiot* at me, wondering why I was ever given these arrows. It's not like my own kids ever give me this grief. I've a good mind to give her a thick...

"It's the one with the green fletches."

"I know," said Kirkgordon, voice low but infused with anger. "I bloody well know."

One of the keys to good archery is controlling your mind and body. Excess stress is often shown in poor shooting and right at this moment Kirkgordon could feel the blood surging round his body in fits of rage. He was anything but calm. So he breathed in deeply and tried to ease the ripples of anger upsetting his peace.

"Are you going to shoot that thing or do you want me to do it?"

"Nefol, shut up."

"She's right, Churchy, you are taking your time over this one," said Austerley, his face feigning disappointment.

"Shut it, Indy. In fact, everyone just shut up until I say so or I'll damn well hit a target closer to me." Kirkgordon looked around, daring anyone to speak. Hearing no dissenters, he relaxed into his shooting stance before loading his bow and then drawing the arrow. For a moment he zoned into a place of contentment and ease, then released the arrow. His head had turned from the shot long before it thudded into the side of Nefol's staff.

"Well, after all that palaver, you are not a bad shot, Mr Kirkgordon," laughed Farthington.

"Shut it," said Kirkgordon. He grabbed hold of the rope that the arrow had produced and it became a solid straight line from end to tip.

"Farthington, you and your lackey can go first."

"Afraid to enter the fray, Mr Kirkgordon?"

"Hardly. But if Nefol goes first, she has no weapon as she can't take her weapon until we are all up the rope. I'm babysitting the great professor and as Bogey's gone home. That leaves you and gorgeous to take point."

"Indeed, Mr Kirkgordon, you are almost rational." With that, Farthington urged his bodyguard to quickly climb the rope. Although it was at a steep angle, the reptile ran swiftly up and disappeared inside the opening. Farthington quickly followed suit.

Austerley hobbled up to the rope and tried to sit on it. Leaning forward, he swung round so that his body was on the underside of the rope. Kirkgordon reached over, pulled Austerley upright and grabbed the back of his collar. Balancing carefully, he slowly dragged Austerley up the rope. Austerley cried out at the pain in his hands from the rope chafing.

"Shush, Indy, you'll have them all over here."

"You're hurting my hands. I'm already down a foot."

On reaching the end of the rope, Kirkgordon threw Austerley into the opening and continued to hold the rope while Nefol sprinted up it. Just as she reached the end, Austerley's head appeared out of the opening.

"Churchy, there's loads of them."

"Who?"

"Frog-men. Farthington's getting killed in here."

As soon as Nefol had her hands on her staff, Kirkgordon entered the opening, squeezing past Austerley's girth. His eyes lit up in horror at the scene in front of him. The corridor was full ahead. Kirkgordon saw bulbous eyes, too many to count, and Farthington's bodyguard being thrown high into the passage wall. He fell back down limply as Farthington roared out his disapproval.

Kirkgordon was aware of Nefol somersaulting over him and landing ahead. Her staff was spinning despite the space limitations and she was already driving her weapon into frog-men heads. Through the masses in the dimly lit corridor, Kirkgordon could see Farthington being set upon and dragged up the corridor.

"Churchy! Frog-men!"

"Yes, I can see that, Indy."

"No, Churchy. Outside, there's bloody frog-men outside as well."

Kirkgordon turned as a frog-man landed inside the narrow entrance. It received a hard boot in the midriff and fell backwards to the air outside.

"Nefol, get behind me!"

"You won't be able to handle them!"

"Shut it and do what you're told."

"You're not my dad."

"No, I'm your boss. Now get behind me."

Nefol dropped a scowl as she snuck behind Kirkgordon and

then drove her staff into another frog-man arriving at the entrance. Kirkgordon now faced the corridor, where frog-men were beginning to charge.

"Churchy, we're screwed!"

"So little faith, Indy!"

Drawing three arrows, all with the same colour fletchings, Kirkgordon quickly loaded his bow. Aiming about four feet away at the ground, he let the arrows fly. On hitting the stone floor of the corridor, each arrow turned into a giant with a club. The great creatures looked dumbly at one another before turning to Kirkgordon.

"Side by side, turn and face the frog-men and then run down the corridor pushing them all back."

The three giants were tightly packed in the corridor but turned straight away and began to run side by side at the frog-men. One fell behind the other two as the corridor was too narrow, but they hit the wall of frog-men like the rugby scrum from hell. Such was their force that they managed to drive the frog-men backwards at a considerable rate.

"Follow them!" yelled Kirkgordon.

"To where?" asked Indy, starting to hobble. "Can you see another corridor?"

"No, but there had better be one! Nefol, come on."

Austerley stumbled along, and Kirkgordon's hand on his collar reminded him of their dash through Moscow. There he had also struggled for breath and balance, and here and now it was just the same. At times he almost fell to the floor and needed Kirkgordon to hold him upright – well, above the floor, anyway.

The corridor twisted round a corner and the good work done by the giants was beginning to become less effective. Their progress was halted and one of the front two giants succumbed to the frog-men, disappearing in a puff of smoke. Kirkgordon scanned for options. He could see a door in the corridor, on the left-hand side about five metres beyond the front line. Behind him he heard Nefol shout out that the rear guard were catching up on them. He drew another arrow and lobbed it gently over the head of his giants.

Tiny men appeared and began to clamber over the frog-men, causing them to fall over. The giants drove at them with renewed vigour and pushed the tide back further. The door was suddenly exposed and within reach. Nefol cried out from behind and Kirkgordon saw her taking on two frog-men.

"Austerley, break that damn door down." Kirkgordon threw a punch straight onto a frog-man's bulbous eye, causing gelatinous gloop to run over his hand. But his prey fell and he turned, looking for an open door. He watched Austerley throw himself fully into the door shoulder first and bounce straight back off it onto the floor.

Kirkgordon strode over and drove hard into the door, almost knocking it off its hinges. Turning back, he didn't wait for Austerley to stand up but simply grabbed him and dragged him on his backside through the opening.

"Nefol, time to go."

She was still driving her white-hot staff into frog-men and Kirkgordon saw it was going to be hard for her to turn and run. He slapped one of the giants on the back and indicated that he was to go to Nefol and bash frog-men from that direction. His arrival bought her precious seconds and she ran through the doorway.

Kirkgordon slammed the door shut and held himself against it. He waved Nefol and Austerley down the corridor but the wooden-legged professor stood up and began to chant.

"Oh heck, here we go. What's he pinching off who this time? Another foot?"

"Get out of the way," shouted Nefol, "he's sealing the door."

Kirkgordon stepped aside past Austerley and watched his partner call out deep guttural sounds and wave his hands in bizarre gestures. The door started to buckle inward as it was put under a large degree of stress from the other side.

"Let's go, Indy!" said Kirkgordon.

"He's not done," retorted Nefol.

The door turned a molten red and seemed to liquefy. Deep swathes of what seemed like lava were swirling round the space where the door had been. Kirkgordon recoiled from the heat but Austerley stood his ground until his chant had finished.

"Been a while since I managed to do that. Not bad though."

"How long will it hold?" asked Kirkgordon.

"Maybe ten minutes, at best twenty. Hard to tell with these things. It's all to do with the density of the wood and if the trees were at any point in contact with a—"

"Indy, MOVE!"

Austerley felt his collar being grabbed again and they raced off down this new corridor. There was a fork ahead and Austerley heard Kirkgordon grunt a direction at Nefol. There was a constant tapping of the wooden leg on the stone floor and the bind that attached the false limb to Austerley was beginning to bite into him. He wasn't sure how long the leg would last.

Nefol was up front but Kirkgordon was leading the way, shouting out which direction to take. After twenty minutes of running they had turned down many corridors, all stone, and passed several doors. But now Kirkgordon had stopped and Austerley fought to get his breath back.

"Hell, Churchy," spat Austerley, "where are we? You seemed to be sure of where we were going."

"I've no idea, Indy."

"What? But you were telling Nefol which way!"

"All I did was make sure there was no pattern or bias in our decisions so that we would be harder to track. I'm damn well lost, Indy. We need a map."

"I'll just see if there's a local stall round here where we can get a guide book, shall I?"

"Don't be an arse. We'll start checking rooms, see if we can get a map for you."

"And if there's none?"

"Well, Dagon's gonna turn up sometime, so I'll use my divining rod to find him."

"What divining rod?" asked Nefol.

"Indy. What else?"

"You can't," pleaded Austerley.

"I must," said Kirkgordon. "But first we need a map. I had hoped Farthington might have an idea about the place but that notion's sailed to the wind."

"Well, that I don't mind. I hope it's the last we see of that bastard."

Meeting the Missus

Calandra exited the scene of her icy destruction of the guards and stepped out into the corridor. Looking back down the corridor, she shook her head and turned instead to the unexplored part of the passage. As she stepped, she could hear tiny cracking noises from the stone floor. She looked down and saw that there were patches of ice forming around her feet every time they touched the floor. But there was no horror in her mind now, just determination.

After striding down the corridor she reached a junction and had to choose left or right. Continuing down the left channel, she soon heard the sound of slapping feet on the stone. Ah, frog-men, and plenty of them by the sound of it. She considered being elusive and taking another path, but a voice inside spoke to her. Why should she run? Why should she cower? Let them come and test themselves on her. It would be no whirling stick of white that they faced but a full-on winter hell.

Calandra ran towards the sound and soon came face to face with her foes. The frog-men looked at her with bulbous eyes and wide smiles. At least, they looked like they were smiling, their faces fixed in a frog's grin. A barrage of noises came from them as they sized up their opponent. And then, as if the realization had come to them all at once, they charged forward, hopping and leaping.

Touching both sides of the wall, Calandra laughed loudly. Frost raced down the walls and turned the corridor into an all-encompassing ice rink. Flippers slipped and frog-men crashed to the ground, skidding towards her until the frost grabbed them and stuck them fast to the ice. Within a minute there was no sound in the passage, the hellish war cries of the frog-men now terminated. And Calandra continued laughing.

Oh, this was good, this was how she was meant to be. Inside she roared with wicked joy and yearned for her next victim. Through her body surged a power she had only had once before. Then, she had been in her infancy, trying to understand what she had been given. Then, it had cost her her dear Ferrean, but now it would be different. Now she was its mistress. They had taken Havers, they had taken the priest and they had screwed up Indy and Churchy. They would pay. And then, when she was done, she would be able to have what she wanted.

Kirkgordon came into her mind, always keeping his distance. He obviously hungered for her but was always reticent. Well, now she would take him for her own. He was weak when it came to claiming his own. But she would forgive him that and they would be together. At last, her desires would be sated.

She carried on along the corridor until it opened up into a small hall. On the left-hand side were portcullises and signs over each doorway. There seemed to be no other way out except to return along her previous path. She tried to read the signs but the language wasn't one she knew, although she could see that some of the symbols in a plain graphic were saying something about caution to be taken with the portcullis.

Laughing disdainfully, Calandra stepped up to the first portcullis and gripped it tight. The metal froze up and shattered, shards dropping to the ground. That was easy. Something bolted out of the now open doorway and took off up the corridor. Another creature followed and then another. Calandra roared with delight before stepping across to every other portcullis and dispatching each with the same joy.

Creatures raced past her, all shapes and sizes, none that she recognized. For a few minutes she stood and watched them race up the corridor. A group of small beetle-like creatures noticed her and ran straight at her. The first, the size of her foot, jumped onto her leg and ripped through her trousers, large pincers becoming evident. Calandra watched as it broke its jaw trying to bite her. As others jumped onto her, she allowed the cold to engulf them and they dropped to floor inert.

Never before had she had such power to wield and so many targets before her. Looking at her hands, she could see right through them and yet such power surged from them. This felt good. She would leave this place now and find Kirkgordon, win him to her side. He could barely resist her before; now it would be impossible. Let him forget that woman of his.

And then she saw it, from the corner of her eye. The slightest imperfection in the air, something that just didn't look right, a blemish in the print, faint and almost undetectable. Turning to it, she let out a cold stream of breath and watched as a creature half her size became visible. It had pincers, a large pointed limb and an almost complete shell with hundreds of tiny feet underneath its body. There were no eyes. It looked like a deformed cockroach, but crystal blue in colour. Probably from my breath, thought Calandra.

It amused her and she watched it for a while as it trundled around her. Without warning it turned and its pointed limb struck out towards her. It struck her skin and she laughed again as the limb seemed to bounce away. But then her head began to sway. Her body convulsed and Calandra collapsed to the ground. Her eyes were wide open but her body couldn't move. She felt herself being grabbed by the pinchers.

The creature started to drag her through the portcullis and into the dark beyond. She tried to freeze up but to no avail. Whatever she tried, there was no part of her body that would function except her eyes, and they couldn't move but just stared straight ahead. But she wasn't afraid. If it tried to kill her, her body would react. She knew this now. Death would bring out the best in her.

The creature dragged Calandra further into the blackness. The area smelt of animal dung and she heard an occasional splash as she was dragged along, so she was sure there were patches of wet around. In this coldest of states Calandra found it hard to feel the finer subtleties of touch but with the power she wielded, who needed them?

The darkness seemed to go on forever and Calandra became aware of walls around her as her feet bounced off them or her hips caught an obstruction. She tried to close her eyes but there was no response from her eyelids. Inside, a terror was starting to grow, doubting she would ever regain movement, but she quashed this by thinking of the brutal destruction she had already caused. She was almost invincible, wasn't she?

The creature seemed to have little purpose other than to drag Calandra along. It was apparently far from its nest or feeding ground and was as bizarre a predator as Calandra had ever seen. Surely there must be some young nearby to feed. No animal would put such effort into dragging a victim this far.

But then it dawned on her. The creatures in the sea had swarmed to where Dagon had appeared on the island. At least, the darker creatures had; the seagulls had flown off. If Dagon was about, then the creatures would start to act on his will. And he would have them gather those he was looking for.

Calandra's bravado now started to evaporate on the inside. The exterior looked as if it had been missing it for the last thirty minutes at least. Motionless and pitiable.

A shaft of light appeared above her head and she was dragged through an opening. In this new corridor, torches lined the walls and there was wet lichen on the floor. She saw frog-men passing by her, all a little wary. She heard voices and as she rolled to one side she saw a line of cells occupied by a variety of creatures, all humanoid and upright. A few grabbed the bars of their cell as she was dragged past, howling at their incarceration. One spat on her. A door opened and Calandra was flung into a cell.

The cell's solid walls contained a pool with a thin edge. Calandra hit the water and sank until she felt her head hit the bottom of the shallow pool. A pair of hands grabbed her head and pulled it above the water. Calandra couldn't spit out the water and was beginning to choke. Her helper turned her around and Calandra coughed away the next few moments. Slowly, Calandra was thawing and she was aware that the hands holding her were female. Her saviour dragged her onto the narrow edge of the pool close to the wall.

"No wonder he's obsessed with you. Some sort of good-looking freak."

Calandra was unsure who was speaking but she decided to go along with it until she could get a handle on the situation.

"Make sure you leave your hands off him. What's wrong, not speaking? Just another part of this hellish parade that professor dragged him into."

Despite the pain she was in, something scratched at the back of Calandra's mind. She had faced a hydra and fought off frogmen and a fully fledged dragon, but this was a foe to surpass them all. Was foe even the right word? This woman had done nothing except struggle to understand her man's troubles. But maybe that was it; she wasn't worthy of him. She was unable to get into that dark layer that had taken root within Kirkgordon.

"Hello, Alana. Enjoying your trip?"

Calandra looked at the woman leaning over her and saw herself looking back. The skin was less pale but there was the long black hair, the full figure – not as trim as herself, muscles less toned but a similar shape. No, the hips were wider. But then, she was a mother. Another advantage she had.

Alana turned away and sat on the edge of the pool. The gown she wore was wet from the waist down and her legs looked cold. Her eyes were heavily bagged and red from tears.

"How long have you been here?"

Alana threw a look that said *What's it to you?* before holding up four fingers and a thumb from her left hand.

"Hours or days?"

"Days! Five damn days!" Alana lowered her head again.

"And before that?"

"Before that I was in the company of that blasted dragonman, but at least he was tolerable. He didn't mistreat me or leave me in a stinking pond like this. But then the frog people came." Here Alana began to shake. "What the hell are they?"

"They're humans."

"Humans!" Alana's face went white. "How? Is that what they intend to do to us?"

Calandra locked down the panic building inside and decided to ease Alana's fears. "No, we're more likely to be a sacrifice."

"A sacrifice? They're going to kill me?"

Damn, thought Calandra, I thought she had realized that. She watched the woman opposite start to judder, sharp sniffs from her nose trying to pull back the calm that was leaving her to be replaced by sheer terror.

"Where is he? Why isn't he here to get me?"

"I don't know where he is," said Calandra, "but he'll be looking for you."

"You've lost him?"

"Well actually, I was attacked, along with Major Havers."

"Havers? He said he was a bastard."

"Probably a dead one by now. He was overtaken by a horde of the frog-men when we were looking for you."

"Oh. But where's my husband?"

"I don't know. But he'll be close. He was with us in the city. Along with Austerley."

"I hope they get Austerley. I hope they take him and sacrifice him for all that's he's done to my family."

Calandra stood up from the water and strode over to Alana, grabbing her by the arm. "Don't ever say that about him. He's a mess and unhinged but he came to help find you. He brought his foot of evil and risked his life—"

"Foot of evil! That's the problem with him isn't it? My husband was a little restless before he met Austerley but he was never involved in this sort of shit! I mean, what is all this stuff? Dagon, dragons, a place that can't exist but does through some sort of wormhole? What is this hell that Austerley has dragged us all into?"

"It's my world, Alana. Welcome to my worlds."

Major Havers Fights Back

Havers hung suspended from the dank, grey stone ceiling. Beneath him he heard the stirrings of the fish in the water. His wrists were bleeding and blood had dripped into the water, causing the frenzy that had started below. His toes were some two feet from the pool and he wondered if the fish could leap. A sudden blur of colour that bit into his leg confirmed his suspicion and he fought hard to shake the creature off. As it fell back into the pool, Havers raised his legs and curled himself up until his feet met his hands. Safe for the moment, but this was no long-term solution.

Sick bastards these frog-men, thought Havers, but then that's my job. Keeping the general public free from these creatures. And free from Farthington. The name cut into his core and he felt his arms tense even more, despite his already compromised position.

His torso was bare and his shoes and socks had been removed. However, he was still wearing his trousers. He laughed. The strain was too much and he coughed strongly, half choking as he fought to keep his lungs working. They should have stripped me naked, he thought, it's almost amateur. In fact they should have killed me right then and there. I'm a Havers and if you don't put us down then you'll be taken care of. We've always been that way.

A picture of a man with a neat moustache entered his head. He had a lithe figure, strong and spritely. He didn't smile much and his eyes were hard and cold. Havers saw the man standing before a pit of fire, holding a gun to the head of a tiny animal. There were voices crying "shoot", but the man's hand shook and the gun remained quiet. And then the animal tore the man apart.

"Father..."

Havers heard the words echo around the small room as his eyes flicked open. All he smelt was the unrelenting fustiness as he gazed at the bland, damp, infested interior. He'd never make his father's mistake. Of his parents, his father had been the more compassionate one, despite being a British agent. A British agent who fell in love with a Russian. A strong woman from Moscow who managed to maintain an affair with his father despite them being on two different sides.

She was gone so often and he had lived mainly with his father. But she had been fervent in her protection of him. And even by the young age that she left him, she had already taught him so much. His mind drifted and he saw snow. It was a small clearing in the woods and she was walking away from him. Beside him were two men he had seen with his mother on so many occasions, men who had given her orders.

Her long, dark hair shook from side to side as she walked and he saw the tremble in her left hand. Never had she shown a moment of fear or worry in all the time he had known her. And then there had been blood in the snow, a deep red that ran into diluted pink as it spread. She had fallen away from him, her face buried in the snow, hidden from the twelve-year-old.

He had been brought up in a world of hiding and subterfuge, death and fear, but this was the first time that he had killed.

Two small darts struck his mother's murderers and they fell quickly. He had lain in the snow for hours with her until he had heard the others, those sent to see what had happened. Twenty-four hours later he had found his way back to the British embassy and was on his way back to home, having lost the only true "home" he had known.

Yes, they had made a mistake leaving him his trousers. In a convolution an Olympic gymnast would have been proud of, Havers twisted until his face was in front of his waistband. Biting into the fabric, he removed a small saw with his teeth. The implement was only three inches long but he skilfully manipulated it as he pulled himself up to the ropes that bound him.

Within minutes, Havers was unbound and holding himself above the pool of carnivorous fish by the loose bindings. He looked around and saw no place to stand in the room. The pool beneath went from wall to wall. The door to the room was extremely solid and had no keyhole or other fixing on the interior. He had no idea how they had got him into his bindings, as he had been unconscious after the attack at the church and when he woke up he was already in them.

Swinging on the bindings, Havers managed to reach the door and give it a strong kick with his bare feet. The sound resonated in the small room and Havers emitted some wild shrieks. Again he kicked the door and repeated his cries. Someone, or something, had to come.

It took some ten minutes of yelling before the door opened. Havers was warned of the action by the sound of bars and bolts being removed. As it opened, Havers kicked the door onto whoever had opened it, trapping that person between the door and wall. The person had bulbous eyes – a frog-man. Havers dropped onto the door and swung a punch into one of those eyes. His body ached from his suspension but he forced all thoughts of pain aside and drove punch after punch into the frog-man. Kicking the wall, Havers swung atop the door as it opened again and he saw the frog-man topple into the water. The liquid became crazily agitated and green foam began to build, but the frog-man didn't emerge from the water. Havers didn't wait to examine this. He swung out of the door into the corridor beyond.

As soon as he landed, Havers was struck by something hard and wet which caused him to bounce into the stone wall of the corridor, cracking his head. Fighting back the grogginess that was forming, he saw another frog-man bearing down on him. As the creature bent over him, he drove an open hand into the creature's throat and felt it break through the skin and into the windpipe.

The creature swiped a webbed hand at Havers' head, but the major didn't let go of his position and he could hear the creature start to gurgle. With a deft flick he used his opponent's weight to turn the creature, and now Havers was on top. With no more air filling the creature's lungs, it died with Havers on top of it. He glanced around as it expired, checking for any others.

There was no one else about but it wouldn't be long before others arrived. Havers had to close his right eye as blood was pouring into it. He felt along his head until he found the wound. Ripping part of his trouser, he fashioned a makeshift bandage and cleared his eye out. Then he reached into the top of his trousers and ripped four thin blades from the fabric. They had flat pieces of metal emerging from either side of the blade at one end. He used these to wrap the blades to his fingertips, two on each hand.

With no idea where he was, Havers knew his first priority was escape. Calandra might be in a nearby cell and he should probably check if he got the chance, but he knew what he really wanted to do. Hunt Farthington. That was what his mother would have done. Complete the mission, and Farthington had always been his mission.

A noise came from down the corridor and Havers ran for the shadows further along the passageway in the opposite direction. Hiding in the dark, Havers felt the cold come over his torso. He had lost blood and was reeling from his latest fight, but he knew he had to control his breathing and his body. The self-discipline that both parents had drilled into him came to his rescue and he found some calm in the situation. It was unnatural and forced but it served its purpose, as the next frog-man passed by the shadow Havers was in and then passed into shadow itself.

Fearing he might compromise himself further by running, Havers crept down the corridor locating several cell doors. Carefully he opened each door but found all cells to be empty. Apparently Calandra was not nearby. Not to worry, he needed no help to escape this place.

As he wandered the corridors, he heard several frog-men but managed to evade their eyes. No doubt they would soon be looking for him. As he waited at a junction of two corridors, Havers could smell something. It was musky, like an animal, but he couldn't see anything. Then it leapt at him from the shadows on his left-hand side. There was only one possible ac-tion, and Havers slashed at the animal with his hand, whipping his blades across its body.

The creature fell and howled out to the night. Damn, thought Havers, that'll bring them running. This time he ran with all he had until he saw a door on his left-hand side. This whole place was a rabbit warren, all doors and corridors. He turned the door handle and stepped inside.

The room was dark, lit only by two inadequate candles. Hanging on the left-hand-side wall were several cloaks, faded in their colour and ripped in places. But they seemed to hold a grandeur, albeit from a long time ago. There was a bookcase in the wall directly ahead, old volumes stacked in a sloppy fashion and stained brown. Many were tied up with cord and most had some loose cord dangling pathetically.

The right-hand side was the darkest area and Havers couldn't see into it. Listening intently, he heard someone breathe. No, that was no human's breath. Without turning his head to the sound, he gently closed the door behind him. He strode confidently to the bookcase and picked up a manuscript. His face was pointed at the cover but his eyes weren't looking, all attention focused on the shadows cast by the candles, waiting for further sounds.

Havers could sense the frog-man creeping up on him. If he was honest, they were rubbish at creeping around with their large flipper feet. The shadows told him the frog-man had raised his arms to come down on him hard and on hearing a sharp intake of breath, Havers swayed under the attack, coming around behind the frog-man. The small blades took out the creature's throat before it stood a chance.

The difficulty of his situation became apparent to him as he looked at the manuscripts. He was in the middle of a maze-like building with no map and unable to read anything around him to find a clue to the correct direction. Taking a cloak off its fixing, he draped it over his shoulders. The covering for his body was good but there was no cover for his head. Kirkgordon had once told Havers about how he wore a frog-man's head to rescue Calandra. Well, needs must, thought Havers.

Havers emerged from the room wearing the amphibious head and almost collided with a small detachment of frog-men passing by. They parted on seeing him and allowed him passage along the corridor. This is more like it, thought Havers. He was still lost, but at least he would have an easier time moving about.

Havers hopped to the next junction of the corridors, careful to let the robes flap out to cover his feet. He felt nauseous and wasn't sure if it was his blood loss or the foul stench inside the head. But there was no time for such contemplation – he needed to get away from this building and back to the town to find Farthington. The attempted rescue of Alana had been too much of a distraction and he would inform Ma'am of her error on his return.

After turning into another corridor, Havers found a number of frog-men travelling along the corridor dressed in similar attire to his own. The leader of this group uttered some croaks and gurgles at Havers. Having no idea what was said, Havers pointed up the corridor and rolled his shoulders. The leader replied and pointed to the back of the group. Havers obediently hopped into position at the rear and followed the group.

Austerley has a Moment

Kirkgordon spat onto the stone floor. "Bloody rabbit warren. How many tunnels and corridors can a place have? It's getting so that I can't even tell if we've gone forward, back, up or down. Bollocks!"

"Can I have a rest then? Seeing as we're as lost as we were two hours ago." Austerley collapsed against the corridor wall, good leg and wooden stump sprawled before him.

"Nefol, you have any ideas?"

The teenager shot a glance over her shoulder that said *idiot* but a simple "no" was the verbal response. Kirkgordon wondered how she was really holding up. It was bad enough that her father had died back in the real world, but now Calandra was missing. I could really do with her now, thought Kirkgordon. Cally was always supportive, always positive with him. She backed him even when it went against her own hopes and dreams. Part of him wished he'd met her sooner, before Alana, but then he felt guilty. Alana was so special. And then he wished he was a Mormon, in Salt Lake City, able to have two wives. No, that would probably go wrong.

Austerley began to snore. Nefol moved to wake him up but Kirkgordon still didn't know where to go so he waved Nefol off her task.

"Do you think she's alive?"

The question caught him cold. Nefol had that sour, disappointed look on her face, tough and annoyed, but beneath it he could see the cracks forming. The poor girl was scared. Well, join the club.

"Don't think, just trust she is."

Nefol tutted at the comment. Used to just ignoring the insults, Kirkgordon was amazed at how hurt he felt by this rejection of advice.

"Hey, don't tut at me, I mean it. You have to trust otherwise what's the point? At the moment we have nothing, not even a direction to run in. So you trust something will come up. Keeps your spirits up, keeps you focused."

"You shouldn't have sent them off alone."

"No. Stop that. I sent her off with the nastiest, excuse my language, bastard I know. None of us would have made a more deadly ally. Just trust, Nefol. There ain't anything else." Lowering his head, Kirkgordon indicated the conversation was finished. He could see the scowl without looking.

Everything up to now had been easy. There had been a trail. From heading to Russia, then England and then the island. Even in Dillingham there had been something to follow. When Farthington took Alana, Kirkgordon had still had a track through the Russian portal. But now he was lost without a course, steering blindly, a ship adrift on the high sea, hoping for land.

Austerley twitched. Kirkgordon saw it from the corner of his eye and he didn't grasp it fully, but there was a twitch in Austerley's leg. The guy can't even rest at peace. Again, he flinched again.

"No mother..."

Mother? Is he dreaming about his childhood?

"Gatekeeper, no! Not my fault, no... Dagon, no..."

Austerley's voice was starting to increase in volume but his eyes hadn't opened. Ignoring Nefol's questioning glance, Kirkgordon hovered over Austerley.

"Sent out, sent out to find... was never my fault... blame Farthington, it was the dragon..."

"Indy, snap out of it, you're getting loud. Wake up, Indy," ordered Kirkgordon, shaking his colleague.

"Sacrifice... he wants sacrifice... Calandra, no not her... other woman..."

Thwack! The slap was delivered with aplomb and Austerley's eyes opened in a flash. They were staring ahead, transfixed.

"Indy! Indy, are you okay?" asked Kirkgordon.

"I saw them."

"Who?"

"The women."

"Dirty dreams, is that all you men can manage?"

"Shut up Nefol! Indy, what women?"

"Calandra. So cold, glorious with her wings unfurled. And another woman."

"What other woman?"

"Don't know her. Never seen her before."

"Describe her."

"Ordinary woman. Not different in any way."

Kirkgordon realized Austerley's view of women was a little different to most men. Unless they had some weird ability or a set of wings he wasn't interested. "What was her shape? Hair colour? Face?"

"Oh. Curved, medium height. Black hair, long to her shoulders, slightly wavy. Sizeable chest..."

"Alana?"

"Unreal," interrupted Nefol. "Is that how you guys identify all women?"

"Green eyes, slight dip on her mouth, right-hand side. Faint scar line across her forehead?" Kirkgordon gave a challenging look at Nefol.

"Yes," said Austerley.

"Hasn't he seen the photograph?" asked Nefol.

"No. With his connections I thought it better he didn't know her."

"I saw them, Churchy, they're in trouble. Sacrifice. They are going to be sacrificed to Dagon."

"Why? I thought he was coming through to here."

"I don't know, maybe they can't open a door." Austerley sat facing a blank wall but his eyes were lighting up. "He must be close though, otherwise I wouldn't be sensing him."

"On your feet then, Indy. We need to follow your instincts." And that's how I know we're in trouble, thought Kirkgordon.

Standing up and balancing on his good leg, Austerley closed his eyes. Nefol looked at Kirkgordon who just stood and rolled his shoulders. After a minute's apparent contemplation, Austerley turned and set off down the corridor.

"Whoa! Don't get carried away there, speedy. Nefol, go up ahead, check the corridor's clear." Kirkgordon watched Nefol brush nimbly past and run up the corridor making almost no sound on the floor. I'm like an elephant compared to her, he thought. And then Austerley could be heard clumping up the passage, his wooden leg striking the stone. We're like the Keystone cops!

The group made slow progress due to Austerley's condition but he was constantly affirming the direction. As they approached a junction in the corridor, Nefol doubled back.

"I thought I heard something up ahead but I can't see anything."

"Okay," said Kirkgordon, "stay with Austerley, I'll take a look." He ignored Nefol's *What are you going to do?* glance. With his back tight to the wall he approached the junction, scanning everywhere. But there was nothing, absolutely nothing. No, wait. There was something. It was very hard to see, just a disturbance in the eye line. Something that was barely visible, something that had disfigured the air. Cautiously he waved the others to him.

"Can you see it?"

"No," said Nefol.

"Yes," said Austerley, "and I can feel it. It's a" – the sound was like a coughing spasm – "which translates to *invisible sleeper*, as it puts its victims to sleep."

"So you know where it is. Show me!" demanded Nefol.

"Right there," said Austerley, "directly across beside the wall edge..."

"Nefol, no!"

It was too late. Nefol ran, staff swirling at the invisible creature. Striking hard with the white hot tip of her staff, she split the stone floor of the passage asunder before suddenly collapsing to the ground. Watching horrified, Kirkgordon looked for any disturbance to show where the creature was now. Then Nefol's limp body began to move along the floor.

"It's taking her back to its lair. We'll never find her if it gets away," said Austerley.

Kirkgordon loaded three arrows and aimed right above Nefol's body. He ignored the disturbing sight of her frame dragging itself along the ground. Austerley's hand gripping tight on his shoulder was also ignored. Breathing out gently, he let his three arrows fly.

Two arrows fell to the ground, but there was a squeal in the air and the third arrow started thrashing about. Kirkgordon ran forward, causing Austerley to lose his grip and topple forward. Kirkgordon took another arrow and repeatedly drove it into the air surrounding the third arrow. He didn't stop his attack until the arrow stopped moving.

"She's not moving. I'm not sure if she's breathing."

"Never mind that, get me up."

Kirkgordon turned and saw Austerley lying on the ground minus his wooden leg, which had become detached and rolled away from him. It was inappropriate but the image was so funny that Kirkgordon burst out laughing, tension draining from him after his frenzied attack.

"This is hardly a time for merriment. That poor girl is in trouble, it's doubtful that she'll wake anytime soon. And with the noise we're making, no doubt some of the frog-men will already be en route to our present location." Austerley reached out for his wooden leg but only succeeded in rolling over onto his front. "Damn this blasted leg!"

Trying to focus his thoughts, Kirkgordon looked away from Austerley and stared at Nefol's face. Her nostrils were flinching slightly and on putting his finger in front of them he found that she was in fact breathing. With that assured, he turned to Austerley, bit his lip and collected the false leg. Quickly he bound the straps onto Austerley and helped him to his feet.

"Maybe I should take the bow if you have to carry Nefol?" said Austerley.

Kirkgordon frowned. "There's no way you are getting your hands on these," he said, tapping his quiver. "You're bad enough with just your hands, who knows what nonsense you could do if armed." Kirkgordon picked Nefol up and threw her over his shoulder. He'd better get her out of this. Calandra would kill him if she knew Nefol had been injured again.

"This way," whispered Austerley as he tore down a new corridor. Following close behind, it dawned on Kirkgordon that Austerley was on point and probably ill-equipped to deal with a fight. Still, we made our noise behind us, he thought, so I've probably got the more dangerous position. Great!

Kirkgordon tried hard to keep his head up, but the burden of carrying Nefol over his shoulder meant that often his head was looking down. Because of this he saw the change in the floor first.

"Indy, what's this stuff we're walking on now?"

"Unknown. But it's not from here."

Okay, thought Kirkgordon. He was getting used to this kind of thing. "So where is it from?"

"I don't know."

If Austerley doesn't know, hell, it must be bad, thought Kirkgordon. The ground beneath had turned black with the occasional piece of grey. Granular in nature, it felt like walking on a synthetic pitch with the false grass stems removed and only the rubber particulates remaining. The strange thing was that the walls seemed to be made of it too. Crumbling, decaying.

"How come you don't know?"

"What am I? Some sort of encyclopaedia?"

"Frankly, Indy, yes! And a deeply occult one at that. Also, how did it get here?"

"I'm guessing the Elder beings." Austerley muttered this as if it were obvious.

"Because..."

"The grey substance has been found at many sites were they

were believed to have existed in our planet's history. It's an amazing plasm that seems to take different forms wherever it ends up. But I have seen this form before."

"Where?"

"Martin's beach. It was left behind when a creature came out of the sea and took many to their deaths. All by a sort of submission."

"Comforting. Did you see the creature?"

"No, I'm not that old, Churchy. It was almost a hundred years before my time."

"So someone had kept the material?"

"No! You're bloody irritating with your questions at times. It was there when I got there."

"A hundred years later?"

"Yes. It's not old when we talk about the Elders. Similar particulates are thought to be over a thousand years old."

"Never tell me your travel company."

Austerley grunted and then stopped suddenly. Processing all that Austerley had said, Kirkgordon didn't notice his colleague stopping and crashed into his back.

"What is it?" hissed Kirkgordon, nearly dropping Nefol.

"There's a door here."

"Where?" Kirkgordon could see nothing. The walls were just like the floor. Black with specks of grey. No lines, no delineation of any kind.

"There," said Austerley and pushed with his hand, causing the wall to move away and reveal a deeper darkness. Before Kirkgordon could stop him, Austerley stepped through the gap leaving Kirkgordon no option but to follow. Inside, his eyes were suddenly blind.

"There have been more than frog-men down here, "said

Austerley. "Someone from our world, at some point."

Kirkgordon wondered how Austerley knew all this but then realized the blinding light was from a modern flashlight. His eyes fought the brightness and he thought he saw shapes on the wall.

"Russian flashlight, Churchy. I reckon Farthington's been here. And this room feels special. Hard to describe why, but it does."

Kirkgordon set Nefol down, propping her against the wall. Austerley turned the flashlight onto the wall and Kirkgordon caught something with his head as he turned towards him. Sharp but heavy, it felt like the edge of desk.

"Just fascinating."

"What is?" asked Kirkgordon, rubbing his head.

"There's a history here. It's very old writing and a lot of pictures. I think it tells about the Elders and also about…"

"Who?"

"Dagon. It seems there's a connection from here to him. Not one he can cross, apparently the rip between the two worlds has fallen apart, but there is still a small hole remaining, about the width of a person. And they… and this I didn't know… they feed people to Dagon. I never realized he had this sort of sustenance. That's why he wants us here. To lure us through the hole."

"Okay, Indy, does it say who goes through the hole, or where the prisoners are kept?"

"No, but it does say they bring them to the void. And it gives us directions."

"And can you read them?"

"Of course I can. Mostly."

"Okay then, time to go find it."

"What about Nefol?"

"She'll have to take a back seat this time. I've a feeling there might be trouble."

The Women

Calandra heard the cell door open and instinctively moved herself in front of Alana. Her companion was shaking with cold and had become rather pale. The cold didn't bother Calandra – it was part of her. She wished she could reproduce the ice that had formed her entire body and see her way out of here, but no matter what she did, it wasn't forthcoming.

The women had been quiet after their initial swipes at each other and they had taken to simply huddling together. This was more for Alana's benefit as Calandra had realized that the woman was close to having a breakdown. *I thought she'd have been stronger somehow,* thought Calandra, especially mentally. *In her sleep she's muttering about her kids or Churchy half the time. It's going to be difficult to get her out of here, especially if I can't get my ice back.*

A frog-man hopped in through the open door carrying a long stick with a pointed end. He croaked something before prodding Calandra with the stick. She grabbed it, placed it between her arm and side, and twisted violently. The weapon snapped in two and the frog-man hurried out of the room. It re-emerged a moment later carrying a gun.

Calandra found it bizarre that the creature kept checking the trigger and whether its finger was correctly around it. Again it croaked and began to wave the gun from them to the door. Calandra lifted Alana to her feet and helped her to the door. Outside was a cohort of frog-men armed with an array of guns and spears. Calandra allowed herself to be pushed and prodded forward, shielding Alana from any force.

"Where are they taking us?" asked Alana, her frame shaking while her clothing dripped onto the floor. The gown was still so wet as to cling to Alana's legs. A sense of pity ran through Calandra for this broken woman, struggling to merely keep going. *She probably has a right to be angry. A right to curse the world. But she needs to keep moving if she's going to survive this.*

After a few minutes' walk the creatures pushed the women into a small room and then up against a wall. The room was dark except for the torches on the far wall and empty except for two small gowns on the floor. They were multi-coloured but the fabric was fading and numerous threads emerged from them.

One of the frog-men grunted and the door was closed. In the gloom, Calandra watched who she thought was the head of the cohort. A fat, ugly frog-man, especially rotund with slimy skin. She noticed that he was waving at her and pointing at the gown on the floor.

"What's he saying?" asked Alana.

"I think he wants us to put on the gowns."

"Okay," said Alana. She picked up the one in front of her and began to dress in it. The head frog-man went crazy and one of the other frog-men grabbed hold of Alana and tore the gown off her. Then he removed her other clothing before throwing the gown back at her.

"Bloody perverts," shouted Alana while hurriedly dressing

in the gown.

The head frog-man pointed at Calandra. She stood proudly and removed her clothing before picking up the gown. As she quickly dressed she realized Alana was looking at her side.

"Your side... it's like ice."

Calandra nodded. Not everything had returned to normal, then. The frog-man had noticed too and he grabbed Calandra's gown, thrusting a clammy hand onto her side. Satisfied, he grabbed Alana and stuck a hand onto her side. Alana went crazy, hitting the frog-man with everything she had. But he calmly grabbed her throat and began to squeeze.

Calandra's gown ripped open across her back as large black wings exploded from her. She launched a kick at the frog-man's head. It connected and forced him to lose his grip. Two clammy hands grabbed her from behind but were swept away by her wings. Turning, she followed up with several punches to the frog-man's head before she was jumped by five more guards.

Now being held to the ground, she saw the fat frog-man again thrust a hand at Alana's side while holding her throat. Then he threw her to the ground, disgusted. The frog-men exited and threw a bucket of fish into the room.

"What's that?" asked Alana.

"Our last meal, I guess."

"Is there a cooker?"

"Where do you think we are?

"Well, it's not the Ritz. And I don't do raw fish!"

Calandra laughed. "Yeah, I could kill a steak."

Looking at first like she was going to hit Calandra, Alana began to laugh too. "Yeah, this service is rubbish. No smart tablecloths or place settings."

"No table!"

"No table. I'm not sitting on my ass." Alana started to laugh wildly before collapsing on the floor and burying her head in her hands. She drew large sniffs as she fought back the tears. There was a general depression in the air which Calandra could tell was affecting the other woman even beyond their current situation. The walls of the cell had a pungent dankness to them which set the tone for the place.

"Do you know how to make sushi?"

Alana stopped crying suddenly and looked at Calandra. Total incomprehension filled her face.

"Well, we have no fire to cook with so I was just hoping. I mean seriously, we don't know when we will eat again. If you knew how to we could possibly get something to keep us going."

"Keep us going for what?" asked Alana. "Who knows what's next after the froggie perves come back."

"They mean to sacrifice us. They have dragged us here and now are dressing us in identical robes, in clothing that is too unsubstantial to do anything else but be sacrificed."

"And you talk about food. Maybe you should find us a way out of here. After all, you're meant to be the killer who can deal with these creatures."

"Who said I was a killer?"

"He said you killed them. He said you fought well with your staff, far beyond his ability. He said you had special powers and could make people disappear through signs in the ground. So give me a sign to fly through."

"Is there anything he didn't say about me?"

"Yeah," spat Alana. "He didn't say he wanted you. He didn't have to."

Calandra turned away. Part of her was glowing inside at the confirmation of Kirkgordon's feelings for her, but part of her was ashamed. This woman had been brought beyond all things she should know or be involved in, and all she could think about was her husband's potential betrayal.

"Well, whatever I have it's not enough. He chose you, he still chooses you. Do you not think I'd have taken him away if I could? But he wouldn't be him any more if he cheated. He'll always choose you first. Don't you see? It's the one thing I hate about him."

Alana stared at Calandra, her black hair straggled down her back, greasy and knotted. There was anger in her eyes, a raging inferno which begged to grab a victim. It seemed to Calandra that here was a woman who felt life had just been dealing her one crappy card after another.

"First, he can't give up on this protection business. Then Austerley takes him down that hellhole in the States. Then he's dragged back in as they appeal to his better nature and he's thrust in front of you, all boobs and legs with a pair of wings and an ice box to boot. My man was dragged slowly away from me, bit by bit. And then you put my family into the mix. Why can't you freaks just leave us ordinary people alone?"

There was no response to make. Calandra could see how Alana thought like this. They say children bring out a deadlier instinct in a woman than anything else. Mothers always fight the dirtiest and the wildest. But it was harsh to have a go. I can hardly turn my looks off, she thought. And if she knew just what my wings had cost me.

There was a loud cracking noise which made Alana jump. Calandra looked around for the cause but then realized that her hand was like ice and as she had clenched it, it had made a loud crack. That was the thing about Kirkgordon, he was running deep within her. She suddenly thought that maybe Alana wouldn't survive this and she could comfort him when it was all done, become his confidante, his woman. She hated herself for the thought.

They sat in silence, looking up and staring at each other occasionally. The accusation of taking Kirkgordon away from his wife was weighing on Calandra. Every time she tried to deny it, she had to stop herself. Inside she knew it was true, she knew where she wanted to be. And she knew there was part of him that wanted it too.

Still, it may not matter anyway as they were going to be fodder in some sacrifice. Calandra thought of the girl she had rescued from the hydra. She hadn't been wearing these sort of smocks. No, these were different, which surely meant they were destined for something other than a hydra. With the frog-men's closeness to Dagon, Calandra wondered if it might be the demon himself.

She missed her staff. If she had it with her she could take on many more of these frog-men. They would be a handful without weapons or ice. Although her mood had died down from earlier she still wondered about how cold she had gone. Inside there was a voice driving her aspirations, and it reminded her of Austerley's foot. Few people realized the extent of the darkness within her. It seemed that she may be required to call on it for rescue again.

There was a sound at the door and a frog-man hopped in, holding a gun. The face showed an inane grin and he waved the weapon at the women, indicating they were to leave.

"This floor is so cold," said Alana, but Calandra noticed nothing. Instead she focused on this woman who had made accusations against her about her husband. Why shouldn't I have him? She's weak, feeble, he deserves more. There was another voice inside Calandra coming to the fore. Somewhere deep in her mind she could feel the storm brewing, the wind whipping and the snow falling in a crazy blizzard. There was a laugh, cold and cackling.

"Time to deal with her. We'll have him for ourselves. For ourselves, dearie."

Perfectly Viscous

"So you know where you're going?"

"Yes, and by the way I don't see you being able to read any of these languages." Austerley smirked.

"No, but I can read a face and yours is lying." Kirkgordon smirked back. "I'm not complaining, but as I am the one carrying our precious package, I would like to know we are heading in at least some direction and not simply going round and round while our tour guide fails to spot the marks on the ground that I scored into it the last time we passed through. I know that everything looks the same, Indy, but I thought it was only a moral compass you didn't have."

"I was merely reorienting us on the correct path."

"Yeah, right. I thought you were in tune with Dagon, so you should be able to feel your way there, never mind read a map. I hope you're not staying clear of him."

"First I'm too eager, and now I'm shirking. Make your mind up, Churchy."

Kirkgordon reached forward and grabbed Austerley's shoulder. "Alana is probably there. Don't make me late."

He saw Austerley's shoulder shake before the professor tore off ahead, moving his peg leg as fast as he could. Good, at least he's focused, because Nefol is killing my shoulder, thought Kirkgordon. The girl was limp as he carried her but he could hear her breathing. All his medical skill, the first aid he had learnt as a bodyguard, meant nothing in this land with its strange animals and dangers. Maybe Kilon could help, but really it might seem as if they were getting careless with the child.

Kirkgordon was feeling exposed. His team was shot to pieces: two missing, one down and Austerley the last one standing, which wasn't comforting. He was pretty useless in a fight and likely to go off on a bender if they encountered Dagon. Also, carrying Nefol, his options in a fight were limited, but Calandra would never forgive him if he left the girl behind.

As they edged onward along a new corridor, Kirkgordon thought he heard something. Telling Austerley to shush, he laid Nefol down and put his ear to the ground. At first he heard nothing, but then it became clear. Vibrations were coming through the floor, rhythmic and measured, like a small army unit marching. Except there was a resounding thud each time. No, not a thud, more of a splat.

Kirkgordon signalled Austerley to kneel down and approached behind him. The professor looked distinctly uncomfortable, his wooden leg tucked underneath him, but Kirkgordon had a face that looked like thunder. Confidently, Kirkgordon loaded a brightly fletched arrow and drew his bow. He knew the little men that would come alive would fight crazily, but against the frog-men they lasted for only one or two creatures before expiring. Glancing back down the corridor behind him in case of a forced retreat, good news was not available. There was a shadow coming up the passageway.

"Indy, we're stuck," whispered Kirkgordon. "If you've got a spell or something then don't be afraid to show it."

"Have you a vortex arrow?"

"All out. It's been a bit of a journey."

"Something's close though. I can feel something."

Kirkgordon looked behind him again and saw a multitude of shadows moving and crossing. Meanwhile, his ears heard the constant splat of frog-men on the move.

"I'd like to say this has been a pleasure, Indy, but it damn well hasn't. I'd say keep behind me but I've got a kid to defend, so for once in your life, give 'em hell." Kirkgordon stood up over Nefol and focused on the corridor ahead, waiting to see the frog-men emerge. He controlled his breathing and settled his body as his mind raced at what was to come.

"Churchy, you might want to look behind you."

"Shush, Indy, we'll get to that soon enough."

"You need to see it now."

"Shush." The frog-men came into view. At the same time Austerley began to chant loudly. Kirkgordon drew the bow and aimed at the first frog-man. His fingers let go of the drawstring and he saw the arrow leave the bow, quivering from the force as it flew. And then the wall between the frog-man and himself turned sideways, blocking the creatures from his party and vice versa. The arrow clattered into the wall and fifty tiny men emerged looking puzzled about what they should do.

"Indy, what are you doing?"

"Behind us!"

Turning, Kirkgordon let out the largest expletive of his life. He saw not one but seven heads all attached to a single body. The creature was red and slimy and it glowed in the darkness of the passageway.

"Move the damn wall between us."

"I can't," shouted Austerley, "I can't control that much of it. Deal with the hydra and I'll keep the frog-men blocked out."

"That's your plan? No, you block the hydra and I'll deal with the frog-men. In fact, block them all."

The hydra was advancing quickly on its thick-set legs and Kirkgordon reckoned it would be on them in twenty seconds.

"I can't, there's too much wall to control."

"Just do it."

Austerley chanted again, his hands sinking into the wall. The hydra was almost upon them when the wall shifted and blocked its first attacking head.

"Good, Indy, keep it up."

"I can't hold it."

"Man up."

"You're asking me to link through atoms in another dimension and change the reality of this one. I can't hold on when too much is being manipulated. It'll lose integrity."

"What do you mean?"

The floor beneath the pair began to liquefy and roll about like the sea.

"Like that. Sorry, I can't—"

Austerley disappeared into the now liquid floor, black and dark blue with occasional spots of brightness. Kirkgordon reached instantly for Nefol but missed her as she sank into the liquid.

"Indy, you—" Kirkgordon's words were lost as he ingested part of the wall, like an acidic liquorice taste, and fought for the air above.

Flopping around in a dark pancake batter, Kirkgordon was turned this way and that by the current. He felt the liquid go up his nose and into his ears as he desperately fought to find the surface. It was similar to being in a swimming pool but with a more viscous substance, and all sounds had become dulled and warped. There was a cry of a beast but it morphed into the call from a faulty tannoy.

His head broke out from the liquid and he gulped air as fast as he could before realizing he was falling back in. A sleek red head with fangs and slanty eyes whipped past his vision. At least Austerley had dragged the hydra into this mess too. Just before he splashed back into the liquid, Kirkgordon saw Nefol bobbing out of the liquid below and flung out an arm towards her. His hand found her collar and he grabbed it tight, hoping that it wouldn't slip clear.

As he went under again, Kirkgordon reached out with his other hand and found an arm belonging to his charge. Now with two hands holding her, he pulled her close and wrapped his whole body around her, including his legs, determined not to let her go again. He felt the liquid still around him and had no idea where the surface was. His breath was beginning to run out and panic began to set in. He could free up an arm and risk losing Nefol, but where would he try to swim to? A dark thought arose. He saw Alana held by Dagon, the demon's dark hand crushing her limp body, and then Dagon throwing her lifeless form onto a pile, to land on another female body. But this one was almost glass-like and had a pair of wings emerging from the back. Dear Lord, no! Help me.

Suddenly the liquid parted and Kirkgordon found Nefol and himself sailing through the air, like they had been launched by a wave. The sudden arrival of the ground came as a shock and his shoulder drove hard into the solid floor. His eyes flicked open to see before him a sea of black, rolling heavily with parts of creatures and people appearing at random intervals. Letting Nefol flop onto the floor, Kirkgordon stood up and found his legs wobbling. As he fought to stand up straight, he heard a croak behind him.

Kirkgordon's hand automatically flew to his quiver and he went to take his bow with his other hand but neither were there. The realization of the loss of his weapons in the dark waters caused a panic as he found himself unprotected. Turning round away from the sea of black, he saw that the corridor the frog-men had come down was intact and three of them were standing before him. He stepped over Nefol and took up a defensive stance, determined to take at least one of them down with him.

The front frog-man hopped forward and swung a curving open hand towards Kirkgordon, who ducked and stepped forward with a low punch into the gut of the creature. With his legs still wobbling, he found little power in the punch and was knocked down by the frog-man's hand as it swept back towards him. Kirkgordon's head cracked off the wall and he tumbled to the ground. The creature stood over him and raised its arms to pound him.

There was a moment of panic and then, strangely, resignation. He'd given it everything but this place was just too much. And now it was time to die, time to move on. But the image of the broken bodies of two women he loved came back again. Sorry, he thought, I just couldn't.

The frog-man's arms were grabbed by a pair of human limbs and a disgusting cracking noise was audible as they were snapped backwards. From his prone position, Kirkgordon saw the body falling away, and then he was splattered by a copious amount of green blood. He heard another body falling to the ground and tried to lift himself up. But it was too much and he collapsed back to the ground.

A pair of human hands grabbed him by his shirt and pulled

his face up into the view of a frog-man's head. A voice called to Kirkgordon, sounding like it was coming from inside a bucket. The features of the frog-man's face never changed. It was all Kirkgordon could do to show a frown of incomprehension. But the voice reminded him of someone. Wasn't it saying "Mr Kirkgordon"?

The frog-man's head was suddenly lifted up to reveal a human face with traces of green blood over the eyebrows, hair and moustache. There was no doubting the ruthless eyes that stared hard at Kirkgordon or the urgency of the violent shakes that followed with a repeated question.

"Where's Farthington? Tell me, Mr Kirkgordon, where is Farthington? Tell me or I'll throw you back into that black liquid!"

Havers, thought Kirkgordon, it's bloody Havers. Thank you God, it's bloody Havers.

"He... he went... down... fell beneath a load of... frog-men... when we... came here... at the... entrance..."

"Then I'll be leaving you, Mr Kirkgordon. I'll make sure Farthington is dead and meet you back at the portal if you make it."

"But... Havers... Dagon is... coming through... Alana... Calandra..."

"I haven't seen your wife. Miss Calandra may still be around. I got separated when a sizeable quantity of frog-men attacked us. Good luck, Mr Kirkgordon, but as I said I have a dragon to bury."

Kirkgordon forced himself to sit up and despite his aching head he blurted out what he hoped would keep Havers close. "Austerley knows the way... You're... lost... like me... lost in here... get Austerley..."

Havers' questioning face sought any subterfuge in Kirkgordon's demeanour but he didn't seem to find any. He stepped past Kirkgordon and over Nefol to the sea of black.

"Mr Austerley! Mr Austerley, kindly put the damn corridor back together again. There are things to do."

Kirkgordon turned to see if Havers' words would have any effect but saw only Austerley's arse appear out of the liquid before descending into it again.

"I fear, Mr Kirkgordon, that I may need your help with this one."

One of the hydra's heads appeared from the black mass and snapped at Havers, who delivered a punch to the head. The force of the liquid dragged the head back under and Havers cried out again.

"Mr Austerley, put the corridor back together."

The cry seemed to fall on deaf ears, as there was no reply from Austerley.

"Okay, Mr Kirkgordon, please stand and assist me. When you see Austerley, make a grab for him and we'll drag him onto the solid parts again. Don't be afraid to throw yourself at him, I will catch you."

"And I should trust you? You were about to leave us."

"Indeed," said Havers, "but we both know I need Mr Austerley, so let's not start any unnecessary and emotional ideas. Shall we just get the professor?"

Kirkgordon stood wobbling at the edge of the black sea, watching frog-men, Austerley and the heads of the hydra appear from time to time. Some of the frog-men appeared to have died. Probably suffocated, as the liquid was certainly not water. Austerley was still alive, as evidenced by his occasional shout, but so far was well out of reach. Keeping the focus was hard, but then Kirkgordon saw a hand emerge. He held his breath, shut his eyes and dived into the liquid to snatch the chubby fingers.

Havers had grabbed his ankles and Kirkgordon felt steady within the sea this time instead of swept along by it. Gingerly, he worked his grasp from fingers to hand and then arm. There was a tap on his ankle and he felt himself being pulled hard backwards. With every ounce of strength he had left he clung to Austerley's arm. Then his body, followed by his head, broke free of the liquid and he felt his knees scraping along the solid floor. This stopped when Austerley emerged from the liquid to lie in front of Kirkgordon's vision.

"Ah, Mr Austerley, I believe you know the way out of here. Oh, and I see it's gone. Someone finally carried out my threat. Good. Good to see your foot has—"

"Don't... just don't say that word!"

The Team Back Together

"Where's the wooden leg?" asked Kirkgordon.

"Came off in the liquid. Couldn't grab it," said Austerley.

"What's happened to the liquid?"

"Are you totally stupid? I told you..." Austerley coughed up a solid piece of floor about the size of a marble. "I told you, I was making it liquid, adjusting the atoms with another dimension. Now I'm disconnected it has returned to its normal state."

Looking at where the liquid had been, Kirkgordon saw a few hydra heads and a couple of frog-men limbs. They were encased in the wall material which had now formed a solid sea, seemingly caught mid-wave. The far end of this mass had blocked the previous exit, a complete solid wave covering where the exit had been.

"Looks like you're coming with us, Havers. That exit is solid now," said Kirkgordon.

"Hardly, Mr Kirkgordon, Mr Austerley merely has to redo his trick and I'll be on my way."

"Hang on, Havers, there's no way I'm reopening that. The hydra's stuck in there and a few froggies. You have no idea if they are still breathing and angry. And why would you want to go that way?"

"He wants Farthington, Indy."

"But he was killed by the frog-men at the entrance."

"Are you sure about that, Mr Austerley? Positive?"

"Well, no, but he did go down under attack. And if they didn't kill him they'll bring him to Dagon. Either way, Havers, you should stick with us. Dagon's where we're heading."

"Very good then. What happened to Nefol?"

"Ask Austerley. Some sort of invisible creature."

"Mr Austerley?"

Austerley made another of those annoying sounds that Kirkgordon couldn't imitate. Why couldn't everything be named in English?

"It's a basic poison really, Mr Austerley. Have you helped the girl?"

"I'm not going near that," said Austerley standing up on his good leg.

"Hang on, Havers," said Kirkgordon. "You're saying that we can actually help her?"

"Indeed. I forgot how inept you are in other cultures and species, Mr Kirkgordon, my apologies. You simply have to suck the poison out of her head."

"Simply?"

"Yes, Mr Kirkgordon, simply."

Havers took a sharp needle from his finger and inserted it quickly and calmly into Nefol's eye. Applying some pressure to her temples, yellow liquid began to flow from a small puncture. Havers bent down and began to suck out the liquid, occasionally spitting it behind him. Nefol moaned but didn't open her eyes.

"It'll take about half an hour for her to be upright. She'll be tired, but no long-term harm done, Mr Kirkgordon. I do wonder how you have managed without me."

"Just bloody fine, Havers. We can't sit around here for a half hour, so we should move. I'll carry Nefol and you take point. Austerley can bring up the rear."

"Just how am I going to do that? In case you forgot, my wooden leg is stuck in that stuff."

"It's always about your damn leg, isn't it? When we get back I'm personally taking you to the prosthetic clinic and nailing the flamin' thing on myself."

"Piss off, Churchy."

"Gentlemen, I have a dragon to hunt, so stop this inane banter and let us move out. You can take my shoulder, Mr Austerley. Walk up front with me and direct the way."

Austerley glanced at Kirkgordon with a worried frown.

What does he want me to do? thought Kirkgordon. If he'd helped Nefol earlier this wouldn't be happening, the stupid arse. Besides, as messed up as he is, it's good having Havers about. And if he wants Farthington, he can have him.

The party started down the corridor that the frog-men had come from. As they walked, Kirkgordon noticed Austerley's head shaking from time to time, as if he were removing a fly. This became more frequent the further they walked.

"What's up, Indy? You're like a man in a room full of midges."

"Ah yes, Mr Kirkgordon, good analogy, persistent annoying Scottish flies. But I think the fly annoying Mr Austerley is somewhat larger."

"Indy?"

"I can hear him more easily the closer we get."

"Dagon?"

"Obviously!" And then a tut. Nefol had awoken. Kirkgordon placed her feet on the ground and watched as the girl steadied herself. She seemed a little disorientated.

"Can you feel something?" asked Nefol.

"Yes," said Havers. "I think it's the same thing that Mr Austerley is hearing. Being slightly more attuned, he is picking him up more clearly, but we are all suffering."

"It's just so heavy. Depressing. In my dreams it was all so black."

"In what way, Nefol?" asked Kirkgordon.

"Well, you were in charge for one."

Nothing wrong with her sense of humour then.

"And I saw Calandra, and it was snowing. She was standing holding Dad in her arms. He was dead, frozen. And you, Austerley, you were legless."

"I had realized."

"No, both legs. And he had removed your brain."

"Woah. This isn't helpful," said Kirkgordon. "These things ain't real. No point dwelling on them."

"But my brain..."

"Enough, Indy."

"Can you walk, Nefol?"

"Probably..." Nefol fell to her knees, crying. The three men stood for a moment looking at each other before Kirkgordon knelt beside the girl.

"What's wrong?"

"It was Dad. He's dead. He's still dead."

"We know," said Austerley. "We were there."

Kirkgordon rose like a flash and punched Austerley hard on the chin. He glared down at the prone Austerley before returning to the girl. Hugging her tight he whispered "I know" over and over again as she cried onto his shoulder.

"I want Cally," sniffed Nefol.

"I know. We'll find her. She'll be alright."

"How could you possibly know that?" blurted Austerley.

Kirkgordon went to stand but Havers thrust out a hand to stop him. "Mr Austerley, I think Mr Kirkgordon would kindly like you to shut the hell up before he has to hit you again. Although do be advised he may not have to, because I am closer and will hit you myself if you utter one more stupid and inappropriate comment."

Nefol laughed. It was choked with tears but it was hearty nonetheless. Kirkgordon helped her stand and she threw a glance towards Austerley that dared him to speak.

Turning to Kirkgordon, she gave him a kiss on the cheek. "Thank you. I know why Cally loves you. But you're still an idiot."

"Well, with compliments like that how can I fail? Gentlemen, let's join the lady and go find Calandra."

Havers nodded and picked Austerley off the floor. Together they made a bizarre three-legged team but seemed to move at a pace that defied their situation.

"Where's my staff?" asked Nefol.

"Lost along the way. There was a time when the walls became a sea and I lost all my kit too. Sorry. I guess it's kinda limiting for you, fighting wise."

Nefol laughed. "Hardly," she said and delved in her tunic. She produced two small knives and shook them. They extended into blades of some six inches with ornate handles. "Cally was a lot of things before she met you. Don't worry about me, I'm not useless in a fight yet."

Kirkgordon raised an eyebrow but Nefol began to spin her knives at an unbelievable speed. Having always been a man who preferred targeted weapons rather than those which slash and cut, Kirkgordon had never had the speed of hand which those weapons demanded. Instead he had a steadiness of nerve, but he always marvelled at people who could command a weapon used at such pace.

Kirkgordon also caught Havers casting an admiring glance at Nefol's weapon handling. That was a massive compliment as the spy had proven very adept himself at a number of weapons.

The group continued their walk until Austerley stopped at a junction of two corridors. He started to mumble and his hands shook as he looked first to the left and then to the right. After a slight hesitation he walked down the right-hand path, still leaning on Havers' shoulder.

Within fifty metres the corridor opened out into a cavernous space as wide as a football pitch and heading off into the distance. There were still glowing torches lining the way and Kirkgordon wondered how often they had to be maintained. They hadn't seen anyone changing or topping up the torches, and every frog-man group they had met had been of a fighting nature, not a maintenance crew. Surely a building like this would require such a crew?

"How do they keep these lights going? Indy, where are all the maintenance people?"

"Idiot."

"What did you say?"

"I believe he called you an idiot, Mr Kirkgordon."

"What's so daft about that question?"

"It's bloody Arcassia wood. It's not exactly uncommon and it burns for years. If you look at it, the wood seems to be barely burning. They brought it here from the dark places when they roamed these places."

"The Elder ones?"

"Yes. Now will you shut up? I'm trying to concentrate."

"Okay, Indy. Just making sure you are still with us. Keeping the mood light."

"Excellent, Mr Kirkgordon. Now that we are in these cyclopean rooms maybe we should give a rendition of 'It's a Long Way to Tipperary' or a jolly 'Knees Up Father Brown'. Bringing back the old war spirit as we race, or maybe lope, into battle."

"There's no need to be facetious, Havers. But with this oppression we're feeling and Austerley's suffering from, a bit of lightness wouldn't go amiss."

Kirkgordon looked up at the wall beside him. The black stone was still in effect but the scale of the wall was enormous. I mean, thought Kirkgordon, who the hell walked here?

"I did." The voice was low and full of menace.

"Where did that come from?" asked Kirkgordon.

"Where did what come from, Mr Kirkgordon?"

"That voice." Kirkgordon looked at Nefol but she was shaking her head. Havers also looked surprised. But Austerley was bent over, holding his head.

"That's him, Churchy. That's Dagon."

"How's he in my head?"

"You must be starting to become attuned, like Mr Austerley."

Kirkgordon swore. Loudly. He wasn't having that sort of comment. Even the stare from Nefol for his language failed to calm his anger.

"Come save your women, before I rend the flesh from their bones."

Austerley threw a look towards Kirkgordon. Dammit, thought Kirkgordon. He knows we're coming and he's going to be ready.

"How far, Indy? How much further?" Kirkgordon's voice was becoming panicked.

"I don't know, but it can't be far. You're hearing him which means he can't be that far. Also, look at the size of this place. This is from when they used to roam the world. Well, this world, anyway. This place wasn't built for frog-men. The rift must be close."

"We need to hurry then, before it's too late. Before he…"

"Okay, Mr Kirkgordon, I think we have your message. Step it up, Mr Austerley. I have a date with Farthington and I don't want Dagon getting to him first."

The Platform

Calandra watched as they tied Alana's hands behind her back, seeing her wince as the ropes cut in tight to her wrists. Her own arms were then roughly forced behind her back and she felt cord being tightened against her skin. In her eight hundred years this had hardly been an uncommon experience but she always hated the insinuation someone was going to force her into something. Brought up to be a fighter, a usurper, this was a red rag to a bull.

One of the frog-men had a trident and pushed the sharp tips onto Alana's back, making her stumble forward. Falling into line before they forced her, Calandra projected the image of a broken woman but underneath was already working out how many she could take on at once. Being without a weapon may have reduced that number, but it was still a high count.

She watched Alana in front of her, staggering along, a miserable figure. The woman was sniffling, outright crying at times. She seemed so soft, so delicate, and Calandra wondered why Kirkgordon loved her. Yes, her figure was curvy, attractive, but certainly not as honed as Calandra's. She was like any number of women, really. Dark hair, warm eyes, Kirkgordon had once said. But these eyes were scared, panicked and weary. Did she have no spirit to kick back with?

Alana fell to the ground as they walked along the outside

corridor. A frog-man grabbed her and turned her over. He motioned her to get up but Alana continued to lie there. Get up girl, thought Calandra, otherwise he's going to hit you. Better to get up and walk and be ready.

The frog-man prodded Alana again before grabbing her robe by the front and hauling her to her feet. She spat into his eyes and he slapped her hard with the back of his hand. Falling to the floor, Alana rolled in pain before settling to a quiet whimper. There was a croak from the frog-man and two others disappeared to return with a pole. They bound Alana's hands and feet to it and picked up the pole to carry her. They had bound her with her back facing the pole. Calandra knew how painful it was to be carried like that.

The party proceeded and Calandra wondered if Alana had passed out, as she had stopped whimpering. The walls changed to a black stone she didn't recognize and the torch-lit corridors continued. After what seemed to be an hour of walking they suddenly emerged into a vast room. The ceiling was far above them, lost in the dark, and the walls built of that dark stone were smooth and massive. Each brick was at least ten persons high. The scale was enormous and Calandra understood that they were in the territory of the Elder Beings.

Soon there appeared a small door in the wall. Calandra was ushered inside and made to stand before a frog-men dressed in the, at one time, most elaborate clothes. But the purple had faded from his gown, there were threads hanging from his trousers, and the shoes had split. Calandra became aware of a heaviness in the air, a darkness pervading her mind.

She had always prided herself on her strength of mind. In battle she had seen loved ones fall beside her yet still she continued in a cold, methodical manner until the job was done.

But there was something gnawing at her as this buffoon-like priest wafted some incense around her.

Feeling her eyes becoming heavy, she closed them and was taken to a pleasant scene of a bedroom with sun shining outside. There was a balcony beyond and she recognized the back of Kirkgordon, stood in just a short, thin gown. He was watching something at the corner of the balcony out of her view. He was smiling and she saw the cause of his joy as Alana strode across to him, dropped the towel that was wrapped around her and embraced him passionately.

Calandra walked out to the balcony and put herself in their view. She called to him but he turned and pointed at her, shouting "freak!" She put her hands up, trying to block out the view as Kirkgordon continued with an unbridled hated, screaming she was an abomination. Then she spotted Austerley on the beach.

Vaulting from the balcony, she ran to him, but he slapped her across the face with the back of his hand. She looked up to find him kissing a frog-woman. He turned and cried she wasn't enough of a freak, she was trying to be too normal. And then there was a crowd around her. People she had never met were shouting at her as she fell to the sand and curled up into a ball. Was there nowhere she was wanted?

Her eyes snapped open to see the elaborately dressed frog-man moving over to Alana. As Calandra tried to push away the visions she'd seen, she heard Alana crying out in pain, calling her a bitch and telling her to stop doing that to her husband. Calandra knew what was happening, she knew this was a drug to enhance the despair caused by Dagon's presence, but all she could think was that she could let Alana go to her doom, escape and take Kirkgordon for herself. She would be free to have him and they would both be free of this snivelling bitch before her.

The frog-man indicated it was time to go. Calandra walked past Alana, who suddenly reached out with her head and bit down hard on Calandra's ankle. Kicking with her other foot, Calandra broke the attachment and dropped to her knees before head-butting Alana, drilling her head onto the stone floor. Two frog-men grabbed her arms and threw her out of the door but as she looked back she saw the blood flowing from Alana's head and the indented cheek bone. She didn't care.

The frog-men took them further along the vast corridor until they came to a cut-through passage. Here the passage was dark but there was a light at the far end. Prodded forward, Calandra walked out of the passage and into an enormous cavern.

Standing on a ledge only a few feet wide she struggled to take it in. Directly before her was a wooden structure which led out into open air and which seemed unsupported. Calandra was forced onto the rickety floor and along the framework, which was wide enough for only one person. Cracking and creaking as they walked along it, the wood managed to support their weight until the thin bridge they were on reached some stairs that descended far below.

Looking over the side, Calandra saw a mass of swirling stars which seemed to be slightly veiled. Amongst the stars something moved, swimming about in the void. It was indistinct and Calandra was wondering what it could be until two red eyes stared back at her. Dagon. And again she saw Kirkgordon shouting "freak". Dropping her head she fell into a morose state, complaining about that "bitch" behind her.

The stairs turned in a tight fashion and descended closer and closer to the void below. It seemed an age as they made their way downwards but eventually the stairs ended in a large platform. At the far end there was a post upon which sat a crossbeam with a winding device rigged through it. A rope with a hook on the end hung from the beam. There were barriers around the platform's edges but no supports. Calandra didn't understand how the whole structure was supported but she didn't care. That bitch was going to die and then she would escape and have her man.

The frog-men dumped the women on either side of the platform. They left the women's hands bound but untied Alana from the pole. The frog-men stood guard over them but seemed to be at a loss as to what to do next. Sitting down, Calandra began to formulate her escape plan. She wondered how she could work this so that Alana would be disposed of first. At worst, she'd have to throw her off the platform. The escape back up the structure would be hard but at least she'd only be fighting one frog-man at a time. The narrowness of the structure would see to that. And besides, if things got bad she could always rely on her cold inner persona.

We will have him, my dear. We shall love him, we shall own him. And this excuse for a woman will be gone. Gone! She's not fit to live, not fit to own the name of woman. Calandra listened as the voice continued. It ended with a cackle.

There was movement on the stairs; there were feet involved, and not just webbed ones. The solid stomping sounds were so very different to the hopping thuds. Calandra considered who might be coming. There was no sense of panic from the person, and indeed the simple easy repetition of the gait reminded her of someone. Havers was here! He had made it. Well, he had better fall in line with her plans.

"Miss Calandra. Haven't we got ourselves into a right mess?" A webbed hand slapped her face and Calandra spat at the ground in disgust. Bloody Farthington. He looked a mess. His missing eye was now accompanied by scars all over his face. His right leg had a deep gouge in it and she was sure his left arm was broken. But he retained an upright posture, giving a sense of control.

"I see Dagon is honouring us with his presence today, awfully kind of him really. As an Elder god he must have better things to do. Oh, I see you've met Kirkgordon's woman. Shame she had to be brought into this, but then, if they hadn't have forced my hand at Dillingham... Indeed, if you hadn't been a thorn in Russia, all this would have been very different."

"She deserves to die. And so do you. If Dagon doesn't get you, I'll kill you with her."

Farthington stepped back, a little perplexed. But then he rallied and struck up his arrogant pose again. "Ah, for someone so outwardly impressive you fail so poorly in the mind. Dagon will rip that mind to shreds. You really should learn to control yourself, you could be useful to him, like me."

Calandra wondered what this meant, but it didn't matter. She would take matters into her own hands when the time came, and that time would be soon.

A guard walked over to Alana as the frog-man in the purple robe came down the stairs onto the platform. Calandra watched Alana being taken to the crossbeam and attached to the hook, her hands still behind her. The rope was tightened and Alana was hoisted into the air. Her shoulder blades strained at the weight and she began to scream out in pain. The frog-men ignored her cries for help and swung the crossbeam out from the platform so that she hung over the edge. With a croak of command, they began to lower her towards the swirling mass below.

Redemption

N efol was still struggling and Kirkgordon thought about picking her up on his shoulders for a while but she would probably have resented the implication that she was a child. His own kids were younger and in some ways easier. The whole teenage thing was a complete mystery to him.

"You okay?"

"Yeah, only been poisoned twice so far, so why wouldn't I be? I'm just terrific."

Just when you think you're making a connection, thought Kirkgordon. Anyway, I can't worry about everyone, not this time. I need to get to Alana. First and foremost, find Alana.

Havers piped up to say that there was a tunnel ahead, small, unlike the massive cavern they had been walking in. Kirkgordon pointed onward and then wondered what it must have been like seeing these massive creatures from elsewhere roaming this place. But then he figured that it had probably been pretty dangerous and tried to stop thinking about it.

"I'm here."

The voice was low and rumbling. Austerley must have heard it too, as he threw a backwards glance at Kirkgordon. Watching his compatriot closely, Kirkgordon saw the professor drop his head soon afterwards. He was barely moving. Austerley's inaction was worrying; he was obviously not in the correct frame of mind for what was happening. Dammit, Indy, thought Kirkgordon, I really need you this time.

They walked through the dark tunnel and were flagged down low by Havers as they reached its conclusion.

"This must be where the connection to his world is," suggested Havers. "There's a floating platform of some kind with a few people down there. Well, a few frog-men anyway. From this angle I can't see anything else. She may not be down there, Mr Kirkgordon. And I certainly can't see Farthington."

Austerley had been let down to the ground by Havers but he had curled up into a ball. His shoulders started to shake and he began to choke up. Dammit Austerley, I need you now, thought Kirkgordon.

"Nefol," said Kirkgordon, "see if you can move around the walls and get a better look at who's on that platform. Havers, stay on guard while I sort Austerley out."

Havers took up a position just along from where they had entered. They were on a small crevice but leading away from it was a narrow path cut into the wall. This in turn led across to another tunnel in the far wall and it was from there that the platform structure began with a wooden bridge. A bridge with no supports.

Nefol by contrast climbed onto the vast wall and found a gap between the huge blocks of stone. Her small size and nimble abilities made her a perfect match to scoot along the indentation and she scampered quickly.

Taking a look over the edge, Kirkgordon nearly swooned as he looked into a mass of stars and what he could only think of as galaxies. Far down there was a skin or a transparent surface but nonetheless he felt like he was sitting on a park bench looking out into space. And then he saw something move in the blackness below. There was a wing, talons and then two red eyes.

Kirkgordon saw a large pair of scales in front of him, two blackened pans hanging from a single point by enormous chains. He stared up at them and saw two figures, one climbing to the rim of each pan. One stood upright, looking like an ice figure. He recognized the shapely curves. On the other pan, a broken woman, twisted and ragged, pointed at him.

"You didn't save me. You tell the kids, see how they'll hate you. Murderer of their mother."

Dear God, no, no, thought Kirkgordon. This can't be, it won't be. No! What have I done to her?

It was Alana, but not how Kirkgordon knew her. This was a creature of hate, of anger and pain. This was not the woman he had fallen in love with, married, had two children with. This was not his Alana. Then he saw a staff spin towards her from the direction of the ice woman. He could only watch as it knocked Alana off her pan and she fell into the void below. Kirkgordon thought he heard a cackle.

A blinding light flashed over the pans and there fell from the sky a large man, misshapen with a missing foot. He was bathed in light, shining like the sun through a stained glass window. Austerley!

Kirkgordon opened his eyes in a state of terror and confusion. His mind reeled at what had just happened to Alana. How could he ever have let her become involved in this?

"Churchy, it's my fault," said Austerley. "Dagon's showing me. It's all been me. I'm pathetic. I've no right, no right."

"What are you talking about? Indy, I brought us here. I've lost Alana already. She'll never be the same."

Austerley stared up at Kirkgordon standing over him. "But you always have hope. You always keep going. Dragging my arse here and there, swearing at me and shouting, but you always keep going and see it through. This is from him, Churchy. This is from Dagon. You're not to blame. I got us here."

Kirkgordon turned away at this puerile attempt to pacify him and almost got knocked over by Nefol. She had just jumped back down from the wall, breathless and excited.

"I can see them. There's two women down there, black hair. Two women, Kirkgordon. We've found Cally. I've seen Cally."

Kirkgordon began to lift his head but then laughed coldly.

"We're too late, Nefol. Don't you see, we're too late. I did this to them."

Nefol's face exploded in anger and she shoved Kirkgordon into the wall, before drawing her knives and running for the path to the other tunnel. Ahead was Havers; he had started running too. Kirkgordon watched them go but he had no compulsion to join their efforts. It was all over. All done. He didn't want to witness it.

Austerley grabbed Kirkgordon's leg and pulled hard.

"What?"

"Get me up, get me up."

Kirkgordon cursed but pulled Austerley up and then swore as the professor leaned heavily on him.

"Take me across the path."

"It's too late, Indy, they're as good as dead. It's all point-less."

"Humour me," said Austerley. "For once, just bloody humour me."

Together the world's slowest three-legged team stuttered

its way along the path with a vertical drop beside them of unimaginable proportions. But it was Austerley forcing the pace, despite his impediment, almost whipping Kirkgordon's back with his hand, demanding a faster response.

"Churchy, look. Havers, he's at full sprint for the platform. Look at the bridge. I'd swear that's Farthington. That's bloody Farthington. That means we have time."

"There's no time. There's nothing. Just death. Better to go with her."

"Shut up and keep up. I need to be able to see what's happening. I need to see."

Nefol was running as hard as she could but she couldn't match Havers' pace. She had seen Farthington and realized that he must be about to take part in whatever was going to happen on that platform. The distance was just so great. And there would be frog-men to deal with. But Dad would have done this. Dad would have run into this for anyone, let alone a friend. I'm coming, Cally. I'm coming.

*

Alana had shut her eyes tight when they had swung her out over the drop. Now she could hear the croaks and loud, unholy noises of the frog-men as she descended. It was like that stupid ride she had been on at the fun park. They were both young, only just going together. It had dropped from a height, straight down, lifting her stomach up into her throat. Several times it had gone up and down before coming to a halt. When the restraints were lifted she had thrown herself into his arms. Both mere teenagers, she had only gone on the ride because of him. And then she realized he had known she loathed such rides. His plan had worked, she snuggled deep into his arms.

That had been a time when he was always around her, almost

smothering her with his presence. But she had loved it. After marriage he had gone overseas so often with the job. He was good at protection and she had never truly feared that he would be tempted by the women on the arms of his protectees. But after he quit he had become restless. He meant so much to her but she could never reach that one place. And now it had brought her to this.

Alana opened her eyes and her scream caught in her throat. Below her she saw the stars, the swirling galaxies and the cosmos before her. Her mind saw the thin veil and the small opening she was being lowered towards. Terror ripped through her mind as she saw it through the gap. The talons on its wings, the tentacles from beneath, the red eyes that burned like hellfire. It was as if the devil had just grabbed a hold of her soul.

She shook on her restraints. Her arms screamed in agony as she fought to get back up, to get clear. Then the horror of realizing this was the end gripped her mind. Or was Dagon her eternity?

*

"Stop, stop," yelled Austerley. Kirkgordon halted and Austerley fell over onto the stone floor of the path. Ignoring the pain, he dragged himself to the edge and looked down into the chaos below. In some ways it was beautiful, but he fought to ignore that thought and instead scoured the depths until he saw what he needed.

"Alana, your wife, what weight is she?"

"What?" said Kirkgordon. "What does that matter?"

"It matters! It totally matters. What weight? How much?"

"Ten stone. I don't know. What the hell does it matter?"

"Ten stone," said Austerley. "Ten stone. Allowing for the

transference, taking into account my weight, relative distance, the strength of field activity. Shit, I need instruments, I need some paper."

"Why? What are you doing?"

"Something good before I die. It's not her fault. She shouldn't be there. That's why we came, why I came. I brought him, back on the island, so I need to be the one to face him, not her. He'll only be satisfied with me. I'm doomed. But she's not. She's not."

Kirkgordon watched Austerley start to scrape the stone around him, breaking off bits of dust and stuffing it into his pockets. Over and over he would call out calculations, shake his head at inaccuracies and start again.

"When you get her, run. Just run, Churchy."

"She's gone Indy, she's gone. Stop this. Just stop this."

"Goodbye, Churchy. Maybe you'll think more of me after this."

Kirkgordon watched as Austerley moved his hands in a complex fashion and chanted words that Kirkgordon could never have imagined. Austerley began to change. His complexion took on a grain-like texture and he began to twist. His body spun onto his front and his arms bent backwards. His chest became the only part touching the ground and his body held a shape that it should have been impossible for it to maintain. He screamed briefly before his entire body turned to sand and collapsed onto the path like a child's ruined castle on the beach.

Love Her or Leave Her

Alana stared in horror at the tentacle now emerging from the rift in the star-filled scene below. The surface, whatever it was made of, that separated this place and that below was torn in the smallest of areas, only a few feet wide. But a tentacle, like that of an octopus, was emerging from it. Beyond it, the red eyes of Dagon stared back at her.

There was a judder in the rope. It felt like it had stalled briefly before continuing its descent to oblivion. Something felt wrong. Well, more wrong. Her body felt like it was becoming detached from the situation, like she was drifting away. Alana wondered if this was how the mind coped with unimaginable horror, but there was something tangible in the feeling.

It felt like there was a surface beneath, something solid and cold. And someone was watching her, looking down from above. She tilted her head to look at her body. It was turning into particles. She was cracking up into the tiniest pieces. Alana closed her eyes and tried to scream.

*

Kirkgordon watched as the sand particles began to form a shape again. They rose into a shape similar to that which Austerley had last held, but this figure was more feminine, more curvy than fat. He recognized the curve of that waist and how it swung inward and then out to a chest. Hair began to form, taking on a dark colour. And then the woman that had formed collapsed onto the ground.

Disbelief filled his mind. Austerley had been right there and now Alana had formed right in front of him. He reached down for her, his heart suddenly lifted, and turned her round to see a face that was white with terror. She flung her arms around him and clung tight. He heard her tears, of relief, of joy, and of sheer exhaustion.

"How did I...?" she asked.

"Austerley. He changed places with you. I don't know how, but he magicked you over here. He brought you back."

Alana leant away from her husband to study his face and a sudden look of worry passed across her face.

"What is it? Alana, what?"

She took her left hand from behind his back and counted a thumb and two fingers. Her ring finger and little finger were gone leaving two bloodied stumps. She screamed. Alana began to shake and convulse. Kirkgordon desperately hung onto her and began to make his way over towards the bridge.

"Where are we going? Get me out of here. Get us out of here."

"I am. I'm taking us to safety. Alana, calm down."

"But he'll get us. He'll kill us."

"The others still need me," said Kirkgordon. He threw Alana over his shoulder and began to run along the path but he could feel her still shaking and writhing. "They need me, my team need me!" And the heaviness of thought that had haunted his mind was lifted like a dust cover off a sofa.

*

Nefol reached the bridge at pace and didn't slow down. Havers was ahead of her and had just begun to engage some frog-men who seemed stunned that someone was attacking them. One by one they were thrown over the side by the whirling arms and legs of Havers, moving like a man possessed.

On reaching Havers, Nefol nimbly jumped onto the wooden barrier edge and began to run along it. She passed by Havers, hurdling both the spy and his foe before continuing along the edge. The frog-man would be too heavy for her to throw so she concentrated on getting past as quickly as she could. A quick kick to the head and she was over one. Another felt a blade slash across him as the tiny figure of the girl went past.

She reached the stairs and descended the handrail barrier. A somersault took her past another and she kept running. Not once did she look beyond the wooden structure to the unthinkable drop below. Calandra had taught her well, and now she was totally focused in the moment. Nothing would stop her descent.

*

Austerley was hoping against hope that something might stop his descent. Dagon was staring right at him and he could feel that darkness penetrating his mind. But he also was at peace. It reminded him of his contentment on the island when he had plunged into the water, doomed to spend eternity with Dagon. The worst had happened. But he had a ringside seat at something most people never got to see.

As he stared at the opening below, a thought struck him. He had managed to blend the walls into liquid in the tunnels. What would happen if he could liquidize the rift? Maybe the seal could be momentarily turned to liquid before being shut again. What's the worst that could happen? Well, he could cock it up completely, letting Dagon out into this world and damming it to eternal hell and darkness. But on the other hand, he could stick one over an Elder god. Austerley, the man that messed with Dagon! Doubtless he wouldn't survive, but his legend would.

A tentacle raced towards him from the rift and gripped his waist. It was tighter than any belt he had ever worn and he thought it would rip him in two, but then Dagon wouldn't be able to pull him face to face. Despite the pain, he knew he would reach the rift intact. Timing was the thing now. For once he would have to be on time with his plans.

The tentacle pulled him closer to the rift and Austerley spread his arms out as far as he could. He forced himself to chant despite being dragged downward towards his end. He felt a surge of power like he had never known. He was so close to Dagon's stars that the power he was able to tap was incredible. Even the darkness in his foot hadn't come close. He was going out on a high.

Austerley felt himself touch the edge of the rift and power flowed from him. The solid form of the rift turned to liquid and he felt the tentacle rise and Dagon race upward. And then Austerley's hands were clear of the rift skin and it turned back to solid. The tentacle waved about furiously, shaking Austerley like he was in some giant cocktail maker. But the tentacle didn't descend. It shook and it waved but it didn't descend. He had trapped Dagon.

*

Calandra watched the robed frog-man as he peered over the platform edge. His arms were waving frantically and he was croaking about something. The rope was being winched up in a hurry and she found herself being lifted to her feet. She was prodded over to the rope and her hands were strung up behind her on its hook. The robed frog-man seemed in a panic and was desperate to get her over the side as quickly as possible.

A voice called inside Calandra's head: We'll see her now, see her meet her doom in Dagon's grasp, and then we'll destroy Dagon in a winter's storm, just like poor Ferrean. Then we'll take Kirkgordon for our own. Then he'll be all ours.

The frog-men swung her round on the beam and began to let her descend. She heard a mocking call from Farthington, telling her to pass his compliments to Dagon. But she wasn't truly listening. She was peering down towards the rift, eager to see her foe in Dagon's arms, eager to see her gone from her sight. The rope dropped too slowly for her and she cursed these frog-men with their interminable delays.

Beneath her something was happening. She could see a tentacle with someone in it. The tentacle seemed to be not operating through a hole in the rift but rather it was trapped within the skin between the worlds. And that person that was being swung back and forward was too large for Alana. That was no woman, curved and shapely. Instead it was a hulk of a man, fat with straggly hair. That was Austerley! How was that Austerley?

From inside a rage emerged. She felt her hands start to firm up and go cold. Her body cracked as it was taken over by ice. What the hell was Austerley doing? How did he get there? Alana was meant to have died.

From out of nowhere, snowflakes began to form and a wind began to howl. The vast cavern began to freeze over, sheets of ice forming on its walls. Calandra's mind was filled with hurt and rage. She had lost Ferrean before; she would not lose Kirkgordon.

*

Kirkgordon had succeeded in reaching the far side of the

cavern and set Alana down beside the tunnel. She continued to babble and kept holding him with a tight grasp, refusing to let go.

"We can go, we can get away. C, we can go, leave all this this, get back to our children. We'll be safe there. Hide in our house. Underground, we can live underground where he can't find us with his eyes. We'll be safe, underground. There are no stars underground, no sky for him to come from. Take me there, take me home."

"Alana, stop it. I need to help them. Austerley gave himself for you. Havers is still in trouble. Nefol needs me. And Calandra might still be there."

"Don't you leave me for her. Stay with me. Don't leave me. She'll take you, she'll steal you. Stay with me. Choose me."

Kirkgordon was struggling to get a word in past Alana's ramblings. She was intense and very scared but he needed to help the others. Looking around, he couldn't see any frog-men up on the upper edges and paths and decided Alana would safer waiting here. "Stay here and stay out of sight. Just don't say anything. I'll be back soon."

"Don't leave me," Alana screamed. "Stay."

He turned away to run for the bridge but Alana flung her hands around his legs causing him to trip. As he landed she began to crawl up his leg, nails digging in with desperation. There was only one solution. He placed a hand close to her neck and jabbed a pressure point. Alana collapsed to a silent form. Picking himself up, Kirkgordon took Alana and placed her inside the tunnel. It was narrow but he positioned her in as much shadow as he could.

It struck him what he had just done. Alana was here, needing protection, but he had chosen to leave her exposed while he went to save the others. And he knew it wasn't all the others. Austerley was probably Dagon food by now, and Havers could go swing for it for all he really cared. Yes, Nefol was a concern, but really he was going for Calandra. This was unfair. His mother had once told him that having two women never brought anything good. She couldn't have foreseen this.

Anyway, it was done. A sudden chill filled the air and snow began to form and fall before his face. A wind whipped up and here, far below the ground, in a place it never should have occurred, the mother of all winter storms was forming. He turned to look over the edge and saw a maelstrom of ice whirling above the rift.

His mind shot back to that evening when Cally had spoken of her past. When she had told him about Ferrean. About the rescued children. About the witch and the curse. About how she had killed her own love. And a wild cackle echoed around the cavern filling every part of the void. No, she can't go like this. This will break her. No, no, no!

He ran onto the bridge.

So Long, Havers

Nefol somersaulted and landed on the platform before side stepping a frog-man and catching him across the back with her blade. She scoured the space for Calandra but could not see her. Across from Nefol stood a battered man with one eye missing but a proud gait. Farthington.

"Where is she?" cried Nefol, stepping clear of a swipe from a frog-man's hand.

"Child, they lowered her down after Kirkgordon's wife. I think you are too late."

Nefol raced to the edge and peered over. She saw Calandra descending far below on the rope. Hearing a hop behind her, she side-stepped and a frog-man sailed past her off the platform, giving a hideous croak as he fell. Nefol ducked the next attacker and moved clear of the edge.

The air turned cold and a wind started to blow which swept hard across the platform. As she grabbed the central pole supporting the crossbeam, Nefol felt the wind speed pick up and saw the frog-men struggle to fight against it. One put up his webbed hands and was caught by the wind, sending him flying over the edge. The robe worn by the frog-man conducting the ceremonies inflated and flapped loudly before being carried to the air.

Icicles began to form on the pole and Nefol wrapped her arms around it as her grip started to slip. The platform became like glass, and several frog-man slid past her over the edge to their doom. She saw Farthington lying on the floor, keeping himself as flat as possible as the wind continued. She was stuck now with nowhere to go until this wind abated.

*

The steps were icy and Kirkgordon felt the wind become stronger. He had no weapons to speak of and wondered how he would get past the frog-men to reach the bottom. Realizing he would be blown off the stairs if he stayed upright, Kirkgordon crouched, using the barrier on either side of the stairs as shelter, but he stumbled and half-fell, half-slid down the steps until he crashed into the corner turn where the steps doubled back on themselves.

Again he started and slid over the hard wood covered in ice. He was moving faster than he had imagined and was unhampered by the wind. Turning another corner, he saw a frog-man huddled on the steps below, using the barrier in the same way as him. Kirkgordon slid on his backside and raced down the flight of stairs like a tobogganist who had forgotten his gear. Crashing into the frog-man, they dived down to the corner turn where the barrier gave way, and Kirkgordon desperately flung his hands out.

The frog-man sailed out into the open air and fell. Kirkgordon was left hanging by a hand that was beginning to slip. The wind bit into his skin and he felt the snow melt on the back of his neck. Looking down, he saw the mass of stars and thought this must have been how Armstrong felt. But without the ridiculous balancing act. Sorry, Cally, I tried.

A hand grabbed his. The grip was firm and tight. He found

himself being pulled back onto the stairs, his arm in agony from the stress. Another hand grabbed him and pulled him to the safety of the next flight down and the barrier's shelter.

"Mr Kirkgordon!" shouted Havers. "Too much to do to have you departing so soon. I fear that Miss Calandra is not in a good way and is compromising the mission."

"I doubt this will affect Dagon much."

"Dagon is your mission, Mr Kirkgordon. Farthington is down there and he will pay."

Kirkgordon watched Havers descend the stairs in a half crouch as if the ice wasn't there. His balance was immaculate and a frog-man was dispatched in rapid fashion. Following the spy, Kirkgordon tried to be careful but slid several times, crashing into the barrier. Fortunately his speed was insufficient to break the fixing.

As he reached the bottom of the stairs, Kirkgordon found Havers sheltered and watching like a twitcher in a hide. The subject of his attentions was a man lying on the floor, and Kirkgordon recognized Farthington from the clothes he had been wearing. Nefol was clinging to a pole on the platform.

"Nefol!" shouted Kirkgordon over the wind, "Where's Cally?"

Flicking her head, Nefol indicated over the edge. Kirkgordon saw the rope dangling off the end of the beam and saw that it wasn't moving.

"On the rope, Nefol?"

Nefol nodded. The rope appeared to be frozen, covered in ice. Although it swung from side to side like a pendulum, it wasn't descending. A large chunk of hoarfrost covered the top of the beam and the platform was a mix of snow and ice.

"We need to get that rope moving upwards, Nefol. Can you

get near the crank handle?"

Whether his words were just lost on her or whether she thought his idea was just plain dumb, Kirkgordon didn't know. Either way, Nefol remained gripping the post tightly.

"I can help, Mr Kirkgordon," shouted a prone Farthington.

"Don't trust him, Mr Kirkgordon," shouted Havers. "He's a murderer. Nefol, he killed your father. He deserves to die!"

"And you are not a murderer, Major Havers?" laughed Farthington. "How many dispatched in the service? You and me, Major, we are one and the same. Now we have a common enemy and need to end this portal. I don't think Mr Kirkgordon will let us destroy anything until he has his friends back from down below, so let us put the past aside while we sort out this problem."

Farthington moved onto his knees and started to crawl carefully towards Nefol and the pole, keeping as low as possible to the floor. Kirkgordon saw Havers brace himself before launching forward, sliding across the snow and ice. Barrelling into Farthington, Havers grabbed him tight as they slid uncontrollably towards the edge. Kirkgordon watched in horror as both men disappeared off the platform and out of sight.

*

Austerley was confused by the snow and why he hadn't disappeared into oblivion with Dagon. He was also feeling like he was on an unstoppable fairground ride. And to top off everything, Calandra was now descending from above looking like pure ice. Her body had turned to glass with little frosty patches running across and through it. They always said you can hallucinate at death to ease the pain. This was almost worth it.

Her wings were unfolding behind her and the ties that bound

her snapped loose. Austerley smiled at the woman he had known intimately, with all her glorious strangeness. But his smile wasn't returned and he saw a hate he had never known in her.

"What did you do? Where's his bitch? She was meant to die here."

"Cally, what's wrong with you? You look cursed!" He didn't know how and when, but Austerley, the expert on everything people never wanted to get close to, never mind be an expert of, recognized that something else had taken hold inside Calandra.

"She won't take him from me. They took Ferrean, but no one will take him."

"Who the hell's Ferrean?" asked a bemused Austerley.

Calandra glided up to Austerley using her wings and touched his face. A searing cold gripped his cheek and he felt the moisture lifting clear, his cheek burning. Looking into her eyes, he saw someone else in there, someone he had heard of in the highest reaches of the Alps from a hermit. But she had been only a rumour.

The cold in Austerley's cheek was spreading into his body and he felt himself judder from it. He would be dead shortly if she didn't release her grip. But maybe... he thought about what happened the last time he tried to transfer part of a person. Tania's foot. The young witch's darkness had transferred to him. What could this do to him or Calandra? The hell with it, he would be dead soon if he didn't try.

Reaching out with his right hand, Austerley grabbed Dagon's tentacle that held his waist. With his left hand he grabbed Calandra's hand that gripped his cheek. The power from the rift was strong, there was so much potential in the air, so much flowing through from the closeness of the worlds. Last time he had had to mix potions and bring elements into play but here he could just tap into the energy around him.

Austerley tried to chant but his chin was locked tight. The cold had spread through his face and now he was struggling to articulate any words. He desperately forced his breath out to form the chant. He saw Calandra's eyes grow wild as it dawned on the force inside her what he was doing. His jaw cracked as he forced the words out but he felt a surge of power. This was the way to go out, thought Austerley. Take this, Dagon, you bastard!

The tentacle wrapped around Austerley began to freeze. Although dark already, it took on a new darkness tinged with red which ran along its length, disappearing into the rift. It was followed by a racing cold which froze the tentacle solid. The incessant waving stopped and was replaced by a cracking sound. The tentacle around Austerley shattered and he fell. Got you, he thought as he fell.

Calandra suddenly felt like someone had left her house. Inside, she felt empty. But her instinct took over and she dived down to grab Austerley, catching him just above the rift. With her wings she tried to climb but she was carrying too much weight. Unseen, another tentacle emerged through the rift.

*

On the platform the wind had stopped but the ice remained. Nefol had stood up and was already turning the crank handle for the rope, but the speed she was turning it at told Kirkgordon that there was no one on the end. His heart raced as he wondered what might have happened to his colleagues. Was Cally dead? Is that why the wind had stopped?

The end of the rope appeared and Kirkgordon swung the beam round. Pulling down on the rope he tied it round his waist, knotting it several times. Nefol tapped him on the shoulder.

"I'm lighter, more nimble, let me get her."

"No. I'm stronger."

"But how will I pull you up?"

"I'll climb. I'll get back up." But Kirkgordon had resigned himself that this was probably a one-way trip.

"She's my friend."

"No! Nefol, no. Your father would want more than this for you. I owe him. I owe him my life. So you keep yours."

Before Nefol could speak, Kirkgordon ran and threw himself off the platform. Dumb-ass, thought Nefol. Good thing I have a few tricks up my sleeve. From inside her costume she produced a small glass box. Inside, a small figure with fat arms looked out at its mistress. Strength comes in small packages, her father had said before giving her this for her ninth birthday. She dropped the box and it shattered. Then before her grew an ogre, thick-set with head bowed awaiting instruction. He's built for power, thought Nefol.

*

It was like the worst bungee jump ever. The stars below hurtled up at him and he suddenly realize he had no way of stopping. The rope would reach its end and then rip into his waist or pull the pole from the platform. Beneath him he saw Calandra, wings unfurled, fighting to climb. She was looking up, smiling through her efforts as she saw him. And he was about to smash straight into her.

In sharp jerks he slowed down, his speed eventually reducing to an easy descent, then he came to rest beside Calandra who working hard to stay airborne. Austerley was hanging below her, his collar in her hand. He was shaking with fear but was conscious. Kirkgordon had reached the end of the rope.

"About time," laughed Calandra. There were parts of her that looked like ice but there were also patches of skin, pale and milky white. Her long hair, half frozen, stuck out behind her but she looked magnificent. "I can't hold him forever."

Kirkgordon caught himself and grabbed the rope above him. He shimmied up the rope to leave a loose loop beneath him. Calandra manoeuvred Austerley into the loop and Kirkgordon swung himself through the open loop he had created, tying Austerley into the rope.

Calandra took a hand from Kirkgordon and prepared to beat her wings when the rope moved. Whoever was pulling three people up would require help.

Kirkgordon yelled hard into the cavern, hoping Nefol would hear. His voice reverberated into the silence and he felt the rope flinching. He looked down at Cally's beaming face as she beat her wings. Then he saw the tentacle reach out and grab her round the waist.

In Dagon's Grasp

The tentacle pulled hard. Kirkgordon felt it through his arms as Calandra clung on to his hands so incredibly tightly. The smile on her face turned to panic as the tentacle gripped tighter and the whole rope strained. Kirkgordon held on but they were slowly being dragged down to the rift. If they were pulled through the rift... Dagon had many more limbs to drag them all down to his worlds below.

"Austerley! Have you got anything, Austerley?" Kirkgordon shouted frantically.

Calandra screamed as the tentacle drew blood from her waist. They all slipped downwards. Her wings fought hard but gained no purchase, and the descent continued. Looking all around him, Kirkgordon saw nothing that could help.

Austerley began waving his hands and chanting. For a minute it looked like the rift had changed colour and become firmer. The edges stopped flexing and the descent stopped momentarily. Had Austerley managed to control it? But then the rift ruptured and grew; a second tentacle rushed out of the enlarged gap and grabbed Calandra's legs.

Calandra thrashed in pain as she looked straight at Kirkgordon and cried out, "Let me go! I'm gone, Churchy. Let me go! You'll be safe."

Calandra looked down and saw deep into the space below the

rift. Red flashing eyes passed by and a deep blackness struck all their minds. Right before Kirkgordon's eyes, Calandra began to age and wither, her skin peeling. She looked up, eyes full of terror, and screamed. The rope was at its maximum stretch and there was only a few feet left. Kirkgordon would have to decide, and soon.

Then he saw the change begin. Calandra's arms turned to ice and her face became a torrent of frustrated will. Her wings started to ice up and every part of her gave way to winter. Kirkgordon saw the tentacles go pale and begin to seize up. Dammit, she's attacking him! A crazy-paving pattern grew along the tentacles as they froze.

But then a sharp pain tore through Kirkgordon's arms. Her hands and his own could no longer be seen; a frost had spread rapidly over them and they were now cocooned in ice. The frost ran up his arms and ripped into his shoulders. He looked into Calandra's eyes and he knew what she saw. It was Ferrean happening to her again. She believed she was killing him. And she was probably right.

"Austerley!" There was no other hope, nothing else to call upon. But what could Austerley really do? Then Kirkgordon heard a familiar chant; he had heard it before in this temple. High above on the wall, part of the stonework began to swirl, turning into a tumbling fire. He could feel the heat but its effect was limited. The cold stayed with him and he lost all feeling in his arms. He felt like he could pass out at any moment.

The tentacles suddenly exploded, shattering into a thousand pieces and tumbling into the rift below. Austerley screamed up at Nefol but he was drowned out by an unholy roar emanating from the void.

"Nefol, pull!" he cried, and he felt the slightest upward

movement. Austerley saw the pain on Calandra's face and how she flicked her eyes to break loose the tears frozen on the ducts. But there was no time; he saw more tentacles in the rift below. "Fly, Cally! Beat those damn wings."

Slowly they started to move upwards, a comic connection of hanging fools which began to swing as they climbed. A tentacle shot out but narrowly missed the side of the party before dropping back to the rift below.

"Nefol, faster."

Kirkgordon's arms were still frozen to Calandra. She was staring into a face that was now vacant, his eyes closed. Austerley continued to shout encouragement at her until they were well clear of the tentacles. Then it was quiet while they slowly ascended, dragged by the rope and pushed up by Calandra's beating wings.

Austerley appeared over the edge of the platform and Nefol let out a gasp of relief. With another few turns of the crank handle she was able to swing the beam round and drop her friends onto the platform. Austerley lay exhausted but heard Calandra smashing the ice that bound herself to Kirkgordon.

She cradled Kirkgordon to her bosom, holding tight like a mother to a sore child. Staring in disbelief, Nefol turned and dismissed her ogre, who promptly vanished. There was silence amongst the group until they heard a sound from below.

An enormous roar ripped through the cavern, reverberating around the space and shaking the walls. It brought Kirkgordon round and he sat bolt upright, shuddering at the sound.

"What... what the hell's that?"

"Dagon. I don't think he's happy."

"Thanks, Indy. Don't think I needed an expert for that."

A bolt of lightning ripped through the edge of the platform, shattering the wood and starting a fire. Calandra jumped up and shouted at Nefol to get up the stairs. Moving across the platform was easier with the wind dissipated, but the ice made the path slippery for everyone except Calandra. She seemed at home on the surface and hurried Nefol along.

"Has anyone seen Havers? He went over with Farthington. Is he still here?" asked Kirkgordon.

"We need to go," shouted Austerley, grabbing Kirkgordon's shoulder for support. Haphazardly careering across the ice, the pair fought for footing and desperately lurched for the barrier at the side of the stairs. Another bolt hit the centre of the platform and the pole and beam dropped from their invisible footing and tumbled towards the rift.

"Go, go, go!" yelled Kirkgordon. His arms were burning with cold and were useless. Austerley, minus a foot, grabbed the barrier with one hand and Kirkgordon with the other. Together they climbed the stairs, panting and running for their lives. Nefol and Calandra were skipping up the stairs with a fleetness of foot and reached the bridge well ahead of the boys.

There was a squad of frog-men arguing on the bridge, unsure what was happening and panicking at each new bolt of lightning. They saw Calandra, still covered in ice, her enormous wings unfurled, and a determined-looking child spinning two blades. They decided that today was not a day Dagon was going to win and hopped desperately away from the girls. Nefol ran to attack.

"No!" screamed Calandra. "Track them. We need to find a way out."

The cavern shook again and the stones on the wall began to break and fall. Calandra cleared the bridge and let Nefol track the frog-men. Turning back for the boys, something caught her eye. Alana was slumped in the tunnel, hidden in shadow and apparently out cold.

Although the blackness that had blighted her mind was gone, the memory of all that she had thought still ran through her head, and Calandra stared at the woman who only a short time ago she would have happily allowed to die. Only Austerley's intervention had saved her. She bowed her head, a silent apology she knew Alana could not see, and pangs of jealousy grabbed at her heart. She could not remain around him, not if that was the effect.

A crash and a splintering of wood refocused her mind and she turned to see that the bridge was all that remained of the structure. Her heart skipped a beat. Had the boys fallen?

"Bloody hell, Austerley, get up. Use your arms, mine aren't any use."

"And I haven't a foot, so get up yourself."

Calandra laughed at the continual bickering she had grown used to. It was good to hear them, good to know they were still okay. A blast of lightning caused a rock to fall from the cavern's roof and it demolished the rear of the bridge. Kirkgordon ran forward, Austerley half hopping, half hanging on to his partner's neck, and they tumbled off the bridge and into the tunnel.

Everything started to shake as more lightning raced around the cavern. Bits of wall fell everywhere, throwing black dust into the air, and the tunnel they were standing in began to shake. Calandra reached down and picked Alana up, throwing her over her shoulder. She turned to the boys, threw up a beckoning hand and hurried down the tunnel.

As they emerged from the far end of the tunnel into another cyclopean room, Nefol waved at them from a nearby wall.

"Down there. They all went down holes at the foot of the wall."

"What the hell are they?" asked Kirkgordon.

"Look like possible escape tunnels," said Calandra.

"No, no, no. This is an Elder room, an Elder corridor. They wouldn't use these holes for escape routes, they are much too small. Dagon would never fit down there. It's a storm drain." Austerley saw that the others were looking at him as if he was daft. "It takes the water away?"

"Escape route," chorused the others.

The corridor shook, and lumps of ceiling fell to the floor, launching a black dust storm at the team. Throwing the others to the ground, Calandra threw out her wings to shield them from the debris.

"Damn, that hurt," said Calandra.

"We can't wait," said Kirkgordon. "Nefol, go!"

The girl tucked her arms to her side and jumped into the storm drain. Its sides were several feet from her and she dropped like a stone. Kirkgordon hoped these drains didn't twist and turn like the pipes of a house.

"Take Alana, Cally! Wrap her in your wings," Kirkgordon cried.

Picking up Alana, Calandra did as instructed. She gave Kirkgordon a quick smile and a nod that said *I have her* before leaping after Nefol.

"I don't like water, Churchy," said Austerley.

Kirkgordon's sworn reply was lost to a crash of stonework. His arms still frozen, he head-butted Austerley to knock him backwards into the drain. Without a second thought he jumped after him.

No screams or blood-curdling splats, thought Kirkgordon

as he fell. His arms were numb and flapped around him. One struck the side but he felt nothing. Then he hit the water. He kicked hard to find the surface but felt himself being swept along. Finally his head popped up into darkness.

"Cally?"

His voice echoed around and then he was back under. Again he kicked hard and gasped the air as he felt his head break through the surface. Eyes open, he saw nothing. The water pulled him back down and once more he fought to get above it. This time when he surfaced, there was a green glow around him, apparently from luminous algae on the walls. Austerley's head was some distance away. Kirkgordon tried to call out but couldn't summon enough breath.

A thunderous sound was coming from ahead and he saw Austerley suddenly disappear. The noise was familiar, he had heard it on holiday. Niagara! Bollocks.

He fell into daylight. Pale and weak, but daylight. He crashed into the water sideways and fought to surface. Exhausted, he found himself floating gently in the water until he gradually came to a stop on a sandy bank. The water still flowed across his shoulders but his mouth was clear and he gratefully sucked in air. He fought to lift his head and look around.

Across from him were two legs. One was intact, the other missing a foot. Close by was a cocoon of wet wings. But he couldn't see a child. No, God, I can't lose her. She has to be here. She has suffered enough.

His head was thumping and he tried to ignore the constant and rhythmic banging that was invading his mind. His arms could have been missing for all he knew. All sense of touch was gone, but he thought he could feel a presence. Something familiar. Damn, that pounding.

"Cally," shouted the voice of a teenager, "it's Kilon. Kilon's here! Bogey's come back with Kilon!"

Kirkgordon could feel the relief wash over him. Kilon was here. Bogey had made it back. There would be support and help. He concentrated hard on pushing down at the ground with his elbows to force himself up. It seemed to have some effect but he still felt no sensation.

"Cally, Cally!"

Watching Nefol shout into the face of Cally, Kirkgordon's elation at finding a rescuer was overtaken by anxiety: had the team all made it? He heard a faint flap of wings and his heart lifted. Finally back on his feet, he splashed groggily through the shallow water to Calandra. A grimace greeted him but then it changed to a weak smile.

"I got her out for you. Is she okay?" asked Calandra.

It then dawned on Kirkgordon his first check had been to his friend, his colleague, his temptation. With a guilty heart he quickly moved to Alana but with no feeling in his arms, he was unable to hold her. Instead he crouched over her, seeking some sign of life in her face. This was the mother of his two children, the first real love of his life, and she was barely breathing, her visage as pale as death.

She coughed. Water spurted out in spits and spats and her eyes flicked open. Alana screamed. And then she continued to scream, wild blasphemies coming from her mouth. He couldn't hold her, couldn't comfort her; he felt like a failure. And maybe he was. Was this a rescue? Was this a life recovered?

Hearing someone splashing through the water beside him, Kirkgordon turned and saw Austerley dragging himself across to Alana. As the professor reached her, he placed a hand on her head and uttered some of his unintelligible words. The screaming stopped. There were several splashes and Kilon stood beside them.

"I'll look after her, Professor. You and the Archer need to be helped yourselves."

Kirkgordon turned away but someone touched his leg. It was Austerley.

"You had her. You didn't have to come for me."

"No, I didn't," Kirkgordon replied. "But I had to go for her." He looked over at Calandra, who was beginning to sit up. They were all alive and yet he felt numb. Alana had begged him to leave and instead he had knocked her out and gone back for Cally. He felt bad that he had no remorse, no second thoughts. But for all that he loved his wife, he couldn't have abandoned Cally. Maybe only God knew how to choose between two loves. "Thanks, Indy. You're a decent freak, really. I guess a lot of us don't understand everything about you. Except Alana. I guess she does now."

"I'll help her. She's not gone. Just broken."

"Indy, we're all bloody broken."

Kirkgordon walked a little distance away and stood looking into the dark barren landscape around him. How was this a victory? How was this a success? Dagon had been stopped but he had lost his wife to Dagon, at least her mind. What do I tell the kids?

An arm wrapped around his waist and he looked down into the eyes of his youngest colleague. Nefol was staring into his eyes, searching his pain.

"She'll be alright. Austerley will fix her. We rescued her."

"Maybe. But she's far from saved." Kirkgordon saw Nefol's face fall. The kid had been through so much, she didn't deserve this self-pitying wallowing he was offering. "But as for you...

Your father would have been so proud. Thank you. You helped us all get through."

"Not Havers. Havers didn't make it."

Typical teenager, thought Kirkgordon, always correcting. "I still find it hard to believe. I'd have put money on him being the only one walking back through that portal. Anyway, I'm not sure surviving is all it's cracked up to be."

The Boss

Kirkgordon was happy to be back in Scotland. Even though this was a highland estate that he didn't know and both Austerley and himself had spent nearly an hour blindfolded in the helicopter, it was good to smell the trees after a rainfall. The Nether world had been so strange with its dust and decay, its strange creatures and the overall sense of doom inside the temple. Good, clean Scottish air was a welcome relief.

He wasn't sure why the company had sent them here. Realistically he could have stayed in hospital for a few more days; he had been enjoying the rest. Four months of recovery was a long time and he had feared for his arms at one point. But recovered he had, although with a few "enhancements", as Wilson, who had replaced Havers to become his new boss, had put it.

It was the faint whirr that gave it away. From the outside his right hand looked like anyone else's, but when it moved he swore he could hear it whirring like a machine. The doctor said it was imagined. He was wrong. The damn thing whirred. It had taken a while to get used to and he had crushed a number of glasses en route to his current finesse. But it was good. It worked. Not everyone had been so fortunate.

Alana was still in the psychiatric ward. She constantly felt the darkness coming for her, looking for her. Dagon had gotten into her head and nothing so far had moved him out. One moment she was fine and the next a quivering wreck. She had seen what Austerley had seen, and no sane person could come out of that experience intact. Alana had lost her passion for life, her confidence and her stability. The children were great, Alana's sister was looking after them, but they felt part of Mum was missing. And they were right.

Wilson had been terrific, organizing everything, making sure all the loose ends were tied up. He sent out feelers to places Kirkgordon didn't even know about to try and find out what had happened to Farthington and Havers, but to no avail. They must have died in the temple, but they had never been seen after they fell. Surely someone down below would have clocked them falling into the rift?

Austerley had closed the portal in Russia. It had been a sad farewell for him. Kilon had helped them with patching wounds and had probably saved Kirkgordon's arms. The hand had been too far gone though, its nerves destroyed by the cold. Kilon was a bizarre-looking creature but he had proved his worth. Austerley had hugged him before leaving, in the only genuine sign of affection from Austerley that Kirkgordon had ever seen. Almost moving. Bogey did not participate in the hugging.

From the outset, Calandra had avoided him. Every time she saw his arms she looked away, found an excuse to be elsewhere. Several times she had apologized to Alana but the two women struggled to make up. Alana blamed Calandra and Austerley for what had happened to herself and her husband. Austerley's self-sacrifice had allowed him to avoid the evil eye but for Calandra there was no remorse. It broke Kirkgordon to see the two of them fighting like that.

"Where did you go the other day?"

Kirkgordon flinched as he realized he had been in a different place. He turned to the professor. "Had a guest come to visit. We took a walk."

"A guest?" Austerley chewed the word like a piece of gristle. "Since when has she been a guest? Not even a friend?"

Kirkgordon turned away again. "It wasn't much of a party." He heard Austerley grunt. Good, that's him off the scent. Best he doesn't know. Of course she's more than a guest, but then, she's more than a friend.

When he had met Calandra in London, her hair had been combed long and immaculate, bouncing easily as she turned her head. Long boots ran into bare thighs and some denim shorts. The tight crop top and leather jacket looked like they were part of her. Walking along the Thames, they had barely spoken. He knew she was moving within the department, on to a different side of the work. It was unlikely that they would meet again. For the best, all for the best.

And that should have been it. A handshake and a terse goodbye, colleagues separating until work required them again. But when their hands had met it was with the other's hips. Mouths embraced, a flood that had been held back for so long. And it didn't stop. For ten minutes they had embraced and enjoyed each other. And then she walked away. She couldn't cry; her tears froze as always. But Kirkgordon could, and he had.

"You were too close to work together." Austerley's comment went unanswered.

The other difficult issue had been Nefol. She had wanted to stay with Calandra, but Calandra needed to get away from everything, start again. Her only option was to ditch the hurt and become the Ice Maiden again. It would never work, having a child in tow. So Wilson had come to the rescue again. His friend Miss Goodritch would be good for Nefol. And she was always welcome to visit the boys. In some ways, Nefol had shown the best reaction, thought Kirkgordon. You could see her father in her.

"Is there nowhere here to get a cuppa?" demanded Austerley. Turning around to the little house that was situated at the bottom of the hill, he strode down. The new foot seemed to be working well for him and so far it hadn't attracted any enemies.

Austerley was now part of a secret institute where he could live and research under Wilson's careful eye. Austerley was fed and had various research minions who marvelled at his knowledge and didn't call him an arse and an unwitting destroyer of the world. He has me for that, thought Kirkgordon.

Slowly he followed Austerley along the path to the house made of stone. There was no movement around it but a large Land Rover sat in the driveway. The back door was open and Kirkgordon found Austerley inside the small kitchen shouting for the staff. Whoever manned this place kept it simple. There was an Aga at the rear wall which Austerley was standing in front of, toasting his behind. Atop the old stove was a kettle which was close to boiling, judging from the steam emerging from the spout.

"Ah," said Austerley, "at last, the staff." An older woman in a headscarf had wandered in through the wooden door and pushed her glasses firmly onto her nose on hearing the word *staff*. She almost barged Austerley aside, despite her smaller frame, and pulled down some tea from a nearby shelf. She wore a plaid skirt with a green body warmer and black gloves.

"Austerley, I think maybe we should make the tea."

"Don't see the point when the staff are here. Probably gives this old biddy something to do during her day. Great to see the elderly being put to use, if I'm honest. Lots are just lolling about..."

"Austerley, I think we should make the tea."

"Why? She's making the damn tea!"

"I know, and maybe we should make the tea."

"What's the big deal? She's making..."

"Yes," said the lady, "I am making the tea. If I want to make the tea then I shall make the tea. I think I have a right to, don't you think so, gentlemen?"

"Absolutely, love, you go right on ahead there and do it, don't listen to him," said Austerley.

"Yes Ma'am. Of course, Ma'am," said Kirkgordon.

"Ma'am?" said Austerley, "Bloody Ma'am? She's not the damn Que—."

"Good evening, gentlemen. Now, if you would kindly sit down, maybe we can have some tea?"

"Yes, Ma'am."

Austerley pointed at the woman and mouthed *The Queen?* at Kirkgordon. He nodded. Austerley swore.

"No requirement for the 'F-word', Mr Austerley. Now sit down."

"Yes, Your Majesty. Apologies. I didn't know."

"Indeed. A most unfamiliar face I have. How could you know?"

Austerley sat bolt upright on his seat, staring straight ahead. Kirkgordon was waiting for him to look his way again so that he could laugh.

"Really, Mr Kirkgordon, cut that puerile nonsense out. I thank you for your efforts in the recent foray overseas, so to speak, but I have become aware of a threat closer to home and I require that you both do your duty for this country and, indeed, our world."

"Yes, Ma'am," said Kirkgordon.

"Yes, your holiness... highness, damn."

"Fortunately, I don't require a diplomat, Mr Austerley. I require someone who knows what goes bump in the night and how to deal with it. I take it you still understand these things, Mr Austerley?"

"Yes, Ma'am."

"Good. Because, gentlemen, I think your boat has finally come in. Literally. It's time for you to take a cruise."

"Where, Ma'am?"

"The Bermuda Triangle, Mr Austerley. Have you heard of it?"

"Oh, yes! But I didn't like the Barry Manilow song."

THE END

Bonus: Prologue Book 4

The bar wasn't particularly full but it was cast in shadow from the torches that burned on the wall. He didn't like the contact opposite him, having never worked for him before. Contacts that came via zombies were never good. The zombies never remembered the details about the contact, hadn't a clue what they looked like and invariably the meeting had only come to fruition because the contact had stuffed a piece of parchment with the detail into the zombie's top. Oh yeah, and they were always trying to size up your brain.

But business was business, and when you were struggling to make a living on the "far side", as it was known, you didn't turn away a potential money-making job.

The job in question had involved checking many different hospitals, or rather, "places of rest and recovery", as they were often called. Most of these places didn't advertise their services and didn't take enquiries kindly, so he had had to be discreet. Even then he had almost lost one of his antennae.

The contact opposite was immaculately dressed in an outfit he hadn't seen before. Long pieces of material covered what he thought were legs. The material was grey and black, striped vertically. His torso was covered by a jacket within a jacket with some white material beneath and a black piece shaped like a long triangle. There was black leather on his feet and a black oddly shaped helmet. He also carried a long pointed device which he had been told could expand.

Having watched the contact for a day, he now felt safe enough to part with his information and had delivered a note to the zombie, which had obviously reached the correct source. And now he approached this contact, his first human.

"Did you find what I was looking for?" The contact's voice was strange and he never clicked once during his speech.

"Yes... *click*... I have... *click*... found him."

"And you're sure it's him?"

"Yes... *click*... the eyepatch, the... *click*... scarring of the face."

"Good. Were you followed?"

"No... *click*... I made... *click*... sure."

"Actually, you *were* followed. Easy, it's okay, in fact I intended that to happen. When they corner you and try to find out what you've been up to and for who, you may tell them without fear of reprisal. Please advise them of my name."

"But I... *click*... don't know your... *click*... name."

"Of course. My apologies. It's Havers. Tell him Major Havers is looking for him."

A Small Request

Many thanks for taking the time to read "Dagon's Revenge" and I hope you enjoyed it as much as I did writing the story. As an Indie author, I am constantly seeking to make more people aware of my writing. As such I would ask that if you enjoyed "Dagon's Revenge" please leave a review, on any of your favourite book sites, so others will know about the dynamic that is Austerley & Kirkgordon.

Kind regards,
Gary

About the Author

GR Jordan is a self-published author who finally decided at forty that in order to have an enjoyable lifestyle, his creative beast within would have to be unleashed. His books mirror that conflict in life where acts of decency contend with self-promotion, goodness stares in horror at evil and kindness blind-sides us when we are at our worst. Corrupting our world with his parade of wondrous and horrific characters, he highlights everyday tensions with fresh eyes whilst taking his methodical, intelligent mainstays on a roller-coaster ride of dilemmas, all the while suffering the banter of their provocative sidekicks.

A graduate of Loughborough University where he masqueraded as a chemical engineer but ultimately played American football, GR Jordan worked at changing the shape of cereal flakes and pulled a pallet truck for a living. Watching vegetables freeze at -40'C was another career highlight and he was also one of the Scottish Highlands' "blind" air traffic controllers. Having flirted with most places in the UK, he is now based in the Isle of Lewis in Scotland where his free time is spent between raising a young family with his wife, writing, figuring out how to work a loom and caring for a small flock of chickens. Luckily his writing is influenced by his varied work and life experience as the chickens have not been the poetical inspiration he had hoped for!

You can connect with me on:

- http://www.grjordan.com
- https://www.twitter.com/carpetless
- https://www.facebook.com/carpetlessleprechaun

Subscribe to my newsletter:

- http://grjordan.com/download-footsteps

Also by G R Jordan

G R Jordan writes fantasy books in several series, including the Austerley & Kirkgordon series of which you have just read the third of its origin stories. At the time of publishing there are 3 origin stories and 3 full length novels with more planned in the near future. Published books are detailed below, including the feel good fantasy series, Island Adventures.

Crescendo!: An Austerley & Kirkgordon Adventure #1
A shape-shifting dragon. A cult bringing forth a nightmare. Two broken men, separated by hatred, must bind together to save the world.

Bitter-sweet partners, Austerley and Kirkgordon, take on the darkness to prevent a displaced people ending the world. If you like bizarre creatures, fast paced action and cataclysmic nightmares, you'll love G R Jordan's first novel. Get the book readers have called "a fast paced gothic thriller with lots of humour" and "refreshingly modern take on Lovecraftian themes."

Can the Elder darkness be stopped? It's the blasphemous fanfare for the end of the world!

The Darkness at Dillingham: An Austerley & Kirkgordon Adventure #2

An exhibitionist witch. A English seaside town literally descending to hell. And the only hope is a broken partnership that doesn't want to heal!

"The Darkness at Dillingham" is the second instalment in the A&K urban fantasy series. If you like breakneck action, sexy villains and cutting dialogue, then you'll love this misfit set of heroes. Can the team bind together long enough to rescue a cursed town? Get the book one reader called "A real roller coaster of spookiness with some sexy bits thrown in".

Dillingham, the nightlife's straight from hell!

Footsteps: Austerley & Kirkgordon Origins #1

An insane professor. A journey into a New England grave. Will Kirkgordon return alive?

It was supposed to be a quiet protection job. But under a New England grave yard Kirkgordon meets his worst nightmares. Will he make it out alive with his protectee? Or will he kill him, himself?

Kirkgordon gets his first taste of dark creatures in this first origin story from the A&K universe. If like you like action and adventure, dark creatures from beyond and cutting dialogue from antagonistic heroes then you'll love G R Jordan's A&K urban fantasy series.

Is the real madness above or below the surface?

Cally: Austerley & Kirkgordon Origins #2
A village emptied of its children. A warrior finding her greatest desire. But a witch's vengeance wrecks a curse that will devastate her forever.

The tale of Calandra's curse is the 2nd story in the A&K origins series, a collection of short stories that expand G R Jordan's A&K universe. If you love rollicking action, imperfect heroes and extraordinary, magical villains, then you will love the Austerley & Kirkgordon series.

Yesterday, he offered her the rest of his life. Today a vengeful witch wants to take him away. Can Calandra's dreams survive the mother of all storms?

Sometimes a woman can be too cold for any man!

The People in the Pool: Austerley & Kirkgordon Origins #3

He lost her, murdered a long time ago. But now she's returned. If something isn't real, does it matter?

"The People in the Pool" is the 3rd origin story in the A&K origins series that expand G R Jordan's A&K universe. If you love rollicking action, imperfect heroes and weird villains and places, then you will love the Austerley & Kirkgordon series.

Not every mother can warm a child's heart.

Surface Tensions: Island Adventures #1

Mermaids sighted near a Scottish island. A town exploding in anger and distrust. And Donald's got to get the sexiest fish in town, back in the water.

"Surface Tensions" is the first story in a series of Island adventures from the pen of G R Jordan. If you love comic moments, cosy adventures and light fantasy action, then you'll love these tales with a twist.

Get the book that amazon readers said, "perfectly captures life in the Scottish Hebrides" and that explores "human nature at its best and worst".

Something's stirring the water!